Leaving Emma

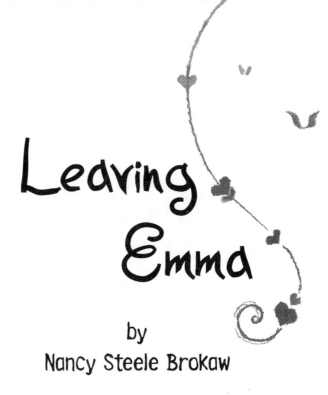

Leaving Emma

by
Nancy Steele Brokaw

CLARION BOOKS/NEW YORK

Clarion Books
a Houghton Mifflin Company imprint
215 Park Avenue South, New York, NY 10003
Copyright © 1999 by Nancy Steele Brokaw

The text was set in 12.5-point Sabon.

Printed in the USA.

Library of Congress Cataloging-in-Publication Data
Brokaw, Nancy Steele.
Leaving Emma / Nancy Steele Brokaw.
p.   cm.
Summary: Fifth-grader Emma faces many unpleasant
changes as her best friend prepares to move away,
her father goes to Turkey for five months, and her mother
starts college, but with the help of her great-aunt Grace,
Emma becomes a lot more independent and self-reliant.
ISBN 0-395-90699-7
[1. Best friends—Fiction. 2. Self-reliance—Fiction.
3. Family life—Illinois—Fiction. 4. Great-aunts—Fiction.
5. Artists—Fiction. 6. Schools—Fiction.
7. Illinois—Fiction.] I. Title.
PZ7.B7864Le   1999
[Fic]—dc21   98-22688
CIP
AC
HAD 10 9 8 7 6 5 4 3 2 1

For my mother, who read to me,
and for Katie and Stephen,
who will never leave my heart

Chapter One

The day Tem made her terrible announcement, I was walking home from school, thinking about painting a picture of yellow leaves stuck to the wet pavement. I was thinking about what color, exactly, concrete was.

When I came around the corner, I saw Tem in our front yard. She was leaning up against the birch tree, peeling away the bark. Most of the leaves had turned yellow, because it was October.

"Why weren't you at school today?" I asked. "Are you sick?"

"Headache," said Tem. "Emma, I've got to talk to you. Alone."

We walked up the sidewalk. I looked at Tem and tried to figure out what she was thinking. I could usually do this. Tem wasn't one of those tricky people.

Tem had been my best friend forever. Her house was in Eagle Crest subdivision, same as ours. Tem's parents grew up in Thailand, and her whole, hard-to-spell name was Sirat Temiyasathit. She was the kind of friend you could say "Shut up" to and she wouldn't get mad. We were always at each other's houses. I knew where they kept their extra toilet paper, and she knew the key-pad number to open our garage door.

"We'll be in my room," I said to Mom, who was lying on the couch reading one of those romance books that have swirly pink covers with gold letters.

"Let's go in your closet," said Tem.

We hadn't gone into my closet for years. I looked at Tem to see if she was kidding, but her eyes were dead serious.

I pushed all the stuff on the closet floor into the corner and shut the doors. It was warm in the closet and it smelled like sneakers.

"What?" I asked, once we got settled. "What's wrong?"

"We're moving," said Tem.

I could hear the faucet dripping in the bathroom.

"What?" I asked again.

"We're moving," Tem said again.

"When?" I said.

"Next summer."

"Where?"

"To Kankakee. It's up north, but it's still in Illinois. Dad's got a job offer, teaching at some junior college. He and Mom have been talking about it, but last night they decided for sure."

If there was something to say, I couldn't think of it.

Tem and I sat on the carpet, in the closet, the light slicing through the door slats in yellow stripes. I looked into Tem's brown eyes and Tem looked into my blue ones. I could hear every drip of the faucet.

"Maybe we can figure something out?" asked Tem.

"Tem," I said in a loud voice, "You're moving from Champaign to Kankakee. That's an awful lot to figure out!"

"I know," said Tem quietly.

It didn't make any sense. I was acting as if I was mad at her. It wasn't her fault that she was moving.

"Maybe your parents will change their minds," I said.

"Maybe," said Tem, but she knew and I knew that her parents never changed their minds about anything.

"Let's play a game," I said. It was starting to feel crowded in the closet. I didn't want to think about Tem's moving anymore. I pushed the doors open, grabbed the Monopoly game, and spread it out on the floor.

It felt good to throw the dice and move around the squares. Everything in Monopoly is neat and lined up—ten squares to a side. For once, I got all the greens and all the yellows. Except I kept telling myself, Who cares? even when I had enough money to buy hotels.

"I better go home," said Tem after a while. Our Monopoly games always sort of fizzled out at the end. Nobody ever won. We liked it that way.

I walked her to the door. A car pulled into the driveway across the street. A boy rode by on his bicycle and a dog barked. Everything was going on outside as usual, as if nothing had happened.

But something had. Tem was going to move, and just the thought of her leaving turned my life upside down.

I shut the front door.

"Time for soccer, Emma," Mom called from the couch.

The last thing I needed right then was soccer practice, but it seemed easier to go than to explain why I was way too upset for soccer.

I rode my bike up to the practice field saying,

"Crap," over and over again. *Crap* is a word my parents never let me use.

"You're late, Emma," shouted Meaghan VanHook. She made this big deal about looking at her watch and using her big, loud voice so the coach would hear.

"Sorry, Coach," I mumbled. I hated soccer. I was one of the worst players on the team, maybe *the* worst. It wasn't hard to figure out. Three of us sat out about ten times more than the rest of the players. Tem's parents didn't make her play.

"I've got new shin guards," announced Meaghan to anybody who would listen. "These are better than the league shin guards—they hook around your feet."

Meaghan VanHook was the most beautiful, talented, intelligent girl at Northpoint Middle School, and if you weren't sure about that, you could just ask her. Meaghan spent a lot of time showing off, and she was another pretty good reason to hate soccer.

Coach Judy put me at midfield. We were having a scrimmage, which was like a real game only worse, because you had to play against your teammates.

The one time I actually kicked the ball, I accidentally kicked it right to Meaghan. With her fancy new shin guards, all sparkly clean in the sunlight, she hauled off and kicked it right over my head and into the goal. Man, I hated soccer.

Back home, I trudged up the stairs to my room. I shut the door and locked it. I pulled my desk chair over by the window. The stars were just coming out in the indigo-blue sky. I stared and stared, but I couldn't find anything to look at.

Tem was moving away. In the summer I would lose my forever best friend. And it wasn't like Tem and I were part of some catchy-named, stick-together group of six girls, like you saw in the movies or read about in books. Neither of us even had a brother or a sister. From the beginning it had always been Tem and me. Nobody else.

Whatever color concrete was, that was the color of my thoughts.

Chapter Two

When Tem and I were little, we would get out the giant dress-up box in my basement and play pretend. Tem would always pretend she was a famous Broadway star. I'd pretend I was something different each time. Once I was Vincent van Gogh with masking tape over my ear. Another time Tem sang "Over the Rainbow" and I wore Dad's plaid shirt and pretended I was Mayor of the Munchkin City, in the county of the Land of Oz.

At school, the day after Tem's terrible "I'm moving" announcement, we played a different kind of pretend. We both pretended Tem had never made her announcement and that things were just the way they had always been and Tem would go on living behind me and everything was just fine.

I didn't talk about it and she didn't talk about it.

We had a spiral notebook that we used only for passing notes back and forth, just between the two of us. We tried to write things in code, in case it ever got intercepted.

We got our math tests back after lunch. Tem got an A– and I got a B+, but we were only two points apart. Tem was smiling, and I could tell she was going to rub it in. She dropped the spiral notebook on the floor between our desks. I dropped a pencil and picked both things up.

I opened to the new page. It said, "I M 2 Y'S 4 U, ha ha."

When Mrs. Beauman wasn't looking, I wrote, "U R B 4 ME, ha, ha."

Pretty much, it was a normal day.

Walking home, Tem and I both talked at the same time. We both talked about school. I guess neither one of us wanted any blank places in the talking where one of us might bring up the big moving announcement. Also, we walked fast because it was cold outside, and Tem had left her jacket at school.

Mom fixed chili for dinner. I could smell it as

soon as I walked into the house. That meant fall was really here. Mom never fixed chili in warm weather, even though Dad and I both liked it.

I couldn't sit still during dinner. I made a fort out of oyster crackers on my place mat. I wanted to tell Mom and Dad that Tem was moving, but I couldn't figure out where it fit in the conversation.

Mom was going on and on about how they had to get the storm windows up *right now* and how they had to get the furnace checked *right now*. I thought about asking, What's the rush? but decided against it.

I put my spoon down and said it almost in a whisper.

"Tem's moving."

They both stopped eating and looked at me. They asked when and where and why, and I told them what I knew.

"Oh dear, oh dear," said Mom. "You two have been best friends for so long. This is upsetting, and I'm not sure I can cope with one more upsetting thing."

What did she have to cope with?

"This will be a big adjustment for you, Emma," Mom went on. "Well, for all of us, really. Think of all the carpooling we've done over the years with Tem's parents. But that's life. Life is full of change. You have to adjust, adjust, adjust."

I bit my lip and held my eyes wide open. I hadn't cried yet, and I wasn't going to start now.

Mom kept babbling on. "Well, let's see, you and Tem can become pen pals. And we can arrange some lovely little visits. Plan ahead, though. Use your people skills and make some new friends, so you're not left high and dry when she leaves. Who knows? You might even find a new best friend."

What could I do? Mom would go on blabbing like this forever if I didn't say something.

"I'll tell you what I think," I said, folding my arms across my chest. "I think you've never *had* a best friend."

That did it. That shut her up. I could see I'd hurt her feelings, and I felt bad. As if I didn't feel bad enough already.

Mom looked at me and looked at Dad, and then she got up and started clearing the dishes, even though half the chili was still sitting in our bowls. Dad picked up his napkin and polished his eyeglasses. He hadn't said anything.

Dad put his glasses on and looked straight into my eyes. I knew he wasn't thinking about a single other thing but me.

"I'm sorry, Emma," he said. "I really am sorry."

He could have said a million things, but that did me in. I ran upstairs and dove onto my bed.

I cried until my pillowcase was wet. Even my pillow underneath was wet.

Sorry was the word. I was sorry, sorry, sorry Tem was moving. You only get one best friend in life. Everybody knew that. And Tem was the BEST best friend on earth. I thought and thought, and I couldn't think of a single mean thing Tem had ever done to me.

I went over to my desk and pulled out a piece of unlined white paper and my Crayola markers. I turned the paper sideways and drew myself on one side of the page and Tem way over on the other side. We were normal sized except for my left arm and her right arm. They were about twenty times too long because they were reaching and stretching across the page, trying to join hands.

Dad interrupted my drawing with a knock on the door.

"Emma, could you come downstairs?" he said. His voice sounded formal, like someone praying at the dinner table.

"Sure, Dad," I said.

I followed him down to the living room. We sat there, Dad and I, opposite each other on the good flowered love seats. I sat up straight, trying to remember if Dad and I had ever sat in the living room before.

"Emma, you know that you and Mom are the

most important things in the world to me, don't you?"

I nodded. What was this?

"This is hard for me," said Dad, "especially with the bad news about Tem."

He picked up a pillow off the love seat and held it with both arms across his stomach, like it was a teddy bear or something.

"I wish I didn't have to tell you this," Dad said.

I didn't like the feeling I had. I felt the way you do right before the scary part of a movie.

Chapter Three

The thing was, in a scary movie, no matter how frightening things got, they were happening to somebody else. This was happening to *me*. I wanted to stop the whole scene somehow, but Dad went on.

"Emma," he said, his voice still sounding formal, "what your mom said at dinner was true. We do all have to learn how to adjust."

"Adjust to what?" He was taking too long.

"I've got to go overseas, to Turkey. Our firm has been working on a big project, and we're way behind schedule. They need an engineer to go over there and stay with the project until it's done."

"How much not done is it?" I asked.

"Quite a bit not done," he said slowly.

"How much?"

Dad sighed. "Five months not done."

"When would you be leaving?" I asked.

"In about a week," said Dad. "I'm so sorry to spring this on you when you're still reeling from Tem's bad news. I thought about waiting to tell you, but I decided it would be better to give you a week to get used to the idea."

His words felt so heavy, I couldn't breathe. I stared at the fireplace.

"Dad," I said, "five months is not an idea I can get used to. That's the longest you've *ever* been gone. I need for you to be *here*. I need to be able to count on you." I wouldn't look at him.

"I'm afraid I have to go. It's my job."

"Find a different job," I said.

"Sometimes I wish I could. I like my job, but I don't like the thought of being gone for so long. Believe it or not, though, you *can* count on me, no matter where I am. We'll just have to ride this one out. Try to do that, will you, honey?"

I had no words. There was a windstorm inside my head.

I left Dad sitting on the couch and went outside and sat on the front step. It was cold, but I didn't care.

The leaves on the trees were trying to hang on, but they were drying up and losing their hold.

They were turning yellow and pinkish red and the color of Dad's good shoes. The wind would blow in the night and scatter the leaves on the ground, leaving the tree branches empty and alone.

Just like me. Empty and alone was the way I felt. Tem was moving. Once she was gone, that was forever. She'd never live a street behind us again. Dad was leaving, too. He'd be back, but not for an awful long time.

Dad had been away working on projects before, usually a couple of times a year, just enough to keep me off balance. Mom and Dad and I would get all settled in a routine and then, bang, he'd be off for some place on the other side of the world that I couldn't even spell. But the longest I could remember Dad being gone was two months. Five months was over twice as long. Five months was forever.

I worried about how Mom would handle it. Sometimes, when Dad was gone, Mom would go into slow motion and not want to do anything but lie around in a warmup suit and watch a movie channel. She'd act like it was a major big deal if I asked her to take me to the art-supply store.

The truth was I hated it when Dad was gone. Everything felt different, and I liked everything the same. I liked coming down the stairs in the morning and hearing Dad complain that the cereal tasted like ground-up trees. I liked sorting the socks into three piles as they came out of the dryer. I liked all three of our toothbrushes sticking out of the blue china cup in the bathroom.

The front door opened. "Emma," Dad said, "come with me. I've got something for you."

I followed Dad upstairs.

"I don't like it when you're gone," I said. I stood on the bed so we were eye to eye. I took the glasses off his face and tried them on, making the room blurry. "Why can't people just stay put? I don't know why Tem's dad had to take this dumb new job, and I don't know why you have to go halfway around the world to help people in Turkey build their building."

"Because Tem's dad is a teacher and because I'm an engineer," he said.

"I need you here, where I can see you," I told him, taking his glasses off my nose.

"I understand, honey," he said. "But I'll be back."

I didn't say anything, because I knew, there in the bedroom with the fading sunlight making pink patches on the floor and my dad so close I could smell him, that of course he'd be back. But I'd been through this before, and I knew that some nights I'd wake up and he would feel farther away than the shadows on the moon. And Tem, once she moved, would probably feel farther away than the shadows on Jupiter.

"I want you to do something for me while I'm gone," Dad said. "I want you to take care of my pocket watch."

Dad's pocket watch was his most prized possession. It had a white face with black numbers. The watch had been his grandfather's, then his father's, then his. Their names were all engraved in cursive on the back, including Dad's: James Ransom Coleman III.

He took it out of his drawer and handed it to me. "We'll set it on Turkey time, eight hours ahead," he said. "That way you'll always know the time where I am. I want you to wind the watch each night before you go to sleep. Twist the knob back and forth three times, like this."

He tipped his head back so he could see the watch through the part of his glasses that made close things clear. "When you wind it, think of me, okay?"

"Okay," I said.

"I'll be back before you know it," Dad said, and he hugged me with my head in the spot on his shoulder where it fit like the last piece in a jigsaw puzzle.

"Take care of Mom, will you? This is hard for her. I'll try and make this the last long trip for a while."

I didn't know how to say what I was feeling, but it was a big feeling, the kind that can make your voice wobble.

"Hurry back," I whispered.

Chapter Four

"What's wrong? Something else is wrong," Tem said as we walked into the school cafeteria. It was crowded and noisy and smelled the way the cafeteria always smelled, no matter what they were serving.

I shook my hair out of the ponytail and let it fall forward into my face. I had decided to grow my bangs out, so my hair was pretty shaggy anyway. Maybe I could hide behind it.

"What's wrong, Emma?" Tem asked again.

"Nothing," I told her.

I didn't want to tell her about Dad leaving. For one thing, she had enough to think about. The main thing was, though, I didn't want to say it out loud. Once I said a thing out loud to Tem, it was real. It was really going to happen, like when I had my tonsils out. I didn't want to tell her about Dad's trip because I was planning on talking him out of it.

"Something's wrong," Tem said for the third time.

Tem always knew. Her shiny brown eyes could see things as they were, like a camera. She never got into trouble with teachers, because she could figure them out. She could figure me out, too.

We were going through the food line and I forgot to tell the server that I wanted *only* ham on my sub. That meant I'd have to pick everything else off.

"All right, you win," I told Tem as we sat down. "Dad's leaving on a trip to Turkey, for five months."

"When is he going?"

"Next Tuesday."

"How's your mom?"

"Okay, so far."

"That's good," said Tem.

I squeezed my juice box so hard, the grape juice squirted onto my denim shirt.

"It's like this," I said. "When Dad's here, he's here. I can always count on him to do stuff. But with Mom, it's different. Sometimes Mom's gone even when she's here. She's not mean or anything, just kind of in her own little TV world."

"You need to know what you can count on," said Tem.

"Exactly," I said.

Tem put her arm around me. "It'll be fine," she said. "Don't worry."

I felt better. Tem was the luckiest thing that had ever happened to me. It was just like her to be all calm and say the right thing. The only time Tem ever lost her patience was around Meaghan VanHook. That didn't count, because lots of people lost their cool around Meaghan VanHook.

Tem stuck carrot sticks in her ears to try and cheer me up. I smiled. It wasn't like her to look so stupid on my account. But the smile didn't go up to my eyes. I didn't have *that* much to smile about.

That night I could tell Mom had gone to extra trouble over dinner. She had set the table with the blue-checked tablecloth. Three yellow candles burned in the center, smelling of lemons. It all looked nice, but Mom's laugh sounded too loud and Dad buttered two pieces of bread that he didn't eat.

"Emma and I will get along just fine," Mom told Dad. "Don't worry about a thing." Her words sounded flat, as if they were in black and white instead of color.

"Everything will be different with you gone, Dad," I said. "A thousand things are going to happen and you won't know about any of them."

"I'll try to call sometimes on Sunday afternoons," he said. "You can tell me then."

Who can remember a thousand things until a Sunday afternoon?

I tried everything I could think of to keep Dad from leaving.

"Hey, Emma," he said one morning at breakfast, "want me to pick up some Styrofoam balls for your solar-system mobile?"

I didn't look up. I kept trying to sink my Cheerios under the milk.

"Emma?" he asked again. "Did you hear me?"

I didn't look up.

At dinner he told Mom that he didn't want any dessert and that he was tired of me not speaking to him. He sounded as though he was mad back at me.

Mom didn't say anything.

On Wednesday, while Mom was at the store, I begged.

"Please, Dad, stay home. Get a different job, and if it pays less we'll sell our house and get an apartment. Maybe we could even move, like to Kankakee or somewhere."

"I've got to go," he said. "Try to remember how much I love you both."

"You don't leave people you love, unless someone like your parents makes you," I said.

Dad ran his fingers through his hair, and I could see shadowy rings under his eyes.

On Thursday I pulled him into the laundry room and shut the door. I told him awful things would happen when he was gone. I told him I had enough problems of my own and I shouldn't have to put up with him leaving, too.

What I told him was the truth.

Dad's response was to tell me to quit exaggerating and come help him pack. He said that nothing awful was going to happen, and I reminded him he wouldn't know if it did.

Dad's suitcases looked big and empty inside. I knew their smell. We filled them up with shirts and pants and shoes. I knew how to stuff socks in the empty corners.

"Hang in there," Dad said when we finished.

I walked down the hall and into my room. I shut the door. I pulled out my desk chair and sat on the edge of it. I was counting on my fingers, over and over again. November, December, January, February, March. Dad was leaving for five full months and a couple of extra weeks. How many days? I couldn't count. We'd get a new calendar before he came back. How many months? I moved my fingers—January, February, March. Three months would go by before he even saw what kind of calendar we picked out.

Chapter Five

Dad left before the sun came up.

At school that day I got into trouble three times for not paying attention.

I kept reading the posters on the classroom walls—as if I hadn't read them a hundred times already. Mrs. Beauman was talking about colorful adverbs as if they were something to get excited about. I just couldn't follow it.

Somewhere, out of a tunnel, I heard Miss Beauman ask, "So, Emma, what adverb do you think would work best?"

"Um . . . 'sadly'?" I stammered.

The whole class, even Tem, started snickering while Mrs. Beauman wrote "sadly" on the board.

The sentence now read, "José laughed sadly at the cat's funny tricks."

Meaghan VanHook whispered so everyone could hear, "Emma has developed a severe behavior disorder."

"Takes one to know one, Meaghan," I snapped back, but I forgot to whisper.

"Mrs. Beauman!" screamed Meaghan, raising her arm so fast, she was lucky it didn't come out of the socket.

After school Mrs. Beauman gave me this big lecture about how important it was to pay close attention. I even had trouble paying attention to her lecture about paying attention.

I guess I was lucky that I had after-school detention for only fifteen minutes. Tem waited for me.

"I hope Mrs. Beauman doesn't put that detention on my report card," I told Tem. "I can't believe I let Meaghan get to me like that."

Tem reached out and grabbed my hand. It was a little-kid thing to do, but I was glad she did it and I didn't let go until we were nearly home.

"Call me," Tem said when we reached my driveway.

The first few days after Dad left on a long trip were usually the same. I knew what to expect when I got home from school. Even out on the street I could see the signs that he was away. All the curtains were pulled and the newspaper was still on the front step. Inside, things felt too quiet. I tiptoed up the stairs and found Mom in bed.

"Oh, Emma, you're home," she said. "Could you get a cold washcloth for my forehead? I've got a migraine."

I let the faucet run to make the water nice and cold. I wrung out the washcloth as hard as I could, so it wouldn't get Mom's long hair wet.

"Emma, could you be a doll and fend for yourself as far as dinner goes? Just the thought of food makes me sick."

"Sure, Mom," I said, and she told me how glad she was that I was such a responsible young lady. I ordered a medium cheese pizza from Domino's and drank grape juice out of a coffee mug.

The next morning I got up early and reheated some pizza in the microwave. I hit the cancel button before the beeper went off so I wouldn't wake Mom. I sat at the kitchen table and drew pictures of loneliness. I drew a dancer on an empty stage, and a duck alone on a pond, and me. I decided to send them all to Dad. Maybe he would feel bad and come home.

Sunday afternoon, October seventeenth, was Tem's birthday party. Tem's mom made her invite all the girls in the fifth grade, even Meaghan VanHook. I'd made Tem and me matching ankle bracelets out of turquoise, hot pink, and yellow embroidery floss. It was the kind of present Tem loved because it wasn't a regular store-bought thing. Nobody at school would have anything like our ankle bracelets, only us.

Three red balloons were hanging from Tem's mailbox. I took my shoes off and placed them, side by side, next to the front door. I could hear voices coming from the family room, including Meaghan's loud one. I wasn't the first to arrive. But I *was* the first to know that placing your shoes next to the front door was the polite thing to do when you visit someone from Thailand.

Inside, Tem's mom had tied crepe paper into bows and taped them all over the family room, across the TV screen, and onto the bottom parts of all the lamps. Most people use crepe paper for streamers, but Tem's mom had her own style.

We all sat in a circle on the floor. Tem plopped down next to me.

"I've got a joke for you," Tem whispered. "It's about olives."

Olives are nasty, so I knew this was bound to be a disgusting joke.

"Knock, knock," said Tem.

"Who's there?" I said.

"Olive."

"Olive who?"

"Olive you," Tem said, and she giggled.

I couldn't help it. I laughed.

My dad loved knock-knock jokes too. Maybe I

could mail Tem's joke to him, in one of those envelopes with the red-and-blue edges. Maybe I could mail an olive with it.

It was a good party. I even won some stickers in a bingo game.

When I got home, I figured Mom would be in bed with a headache, but she wasn't. She was curled up on the couch watching a black-and-white movie.

"Is your headache better?" I asked her.

"Yes, honey. Thanks for asking," she said, not taking her eyes off the TV. "How was Tem's party?"

"Oh, just great," I said. "Of course, it's the last birthday party of Tem's I'll ever get to go to, but it was great." I answered in that tone of voice that means you're saying something with friendly words but you're really angry.

"That's fine, dear," said Mom, keeping her eyes on the TV.

In school on Monday Mrs. Beauman announced we were doing state reports with a partner.

"Tem and I will take North Dakota," I told her.

"North Dakota?" Mrs. Beauman asked. "I don't get many requests for North Dakota."

"My parents were born there," I told her. "It's a big, lonely state."

Tem didn't care what state we did. I told her we'd pick Thailand if we did countries. We both knew how best friends worked.

Meaghan announced she was doing California. By herself. We had twenty-five kids in our class, so one person had to work without a partner. Meaghan thought she was too cool to work with anybody else, and that let exactly twenty-four of us off the hook.

It took Tem and me two weeks to finish with North Dakota. We had to research the official state things like the bird, flower, and song, as well as the state history and what important people came from North Dakota. I drew a page-size version of the state flag that we used as a report cover.

We got out a ruler and measured. The distance from Fargo, N.D., to Grand Forks, N.D., was seventy-five miles. That was the same as the distance from my house in Champaign to Tem's new house, which they hadn't even bought yet, in Kankakee. We'd driven through North Dakota before, to visit my grandma. It was like driving across the moon.

The leaves were really falling, since it was the end of October. It was snowing in colors. Dad and I had always raked the leaves together. Now Mom said cleaning up the leaves was my job.

"Hey, Mom," I said, "since you want me to do the leaves, I was wondering if you'd mind typing our North Dakota paper? It's worth extra credit."

Mom was always up for typing. Before I was born, she worked as a secretary at Caterpillar, which I thought was a goofy name for a big factory.

"Sure," said Mom.

"Want to try it on the computer?" I asked.

"I wish I knew how," she said. "I'd love to be able to move words around and add graphs and pictures. One of these days I'll learn."

"You should," I said. "Anyway, I'll do the leaves and you do the typing."

"That's a deal," said Mom.

I got Tem to help me. We raked the leaves into little piles, and then we raked the little piles into bigger piles and finally into one big pile that we jumped in.

Sometimes when we raked, I could see my dad raking alongside us. Not the way you see people in real life or on TV, but in a different way, sort of inside my head. I needed to remember to tell Dad about this when he called.

That night I found a half-empty notebook and glued a piece of white paper on the cover. I drew a border of pens, pencils and markers. In the center, in cursive, I wrote *Day by Day.* At first I was going to call it *Emma's Journal,* but I thought

"Day by Day" sounded a lot better. I didn't want to write a bunch of words, so that night I wrote just one: *leaves*. If I read that one word, I'd remember the rest and be able to tell Dad.

I wrote down *soccer,* too, because I had sort of, almost, scored a goal, and I figured Dad would want to know. Dad liked soccer a lot more than I did.

After my bath I shut the door and climbed up on my bed. I held Dad's pocket watch in my hand. It felt smooth and solid and the right amount of heavy, like a good rock. I heard the seconds ticking out the time. Time was falling away, like leaves blowing to the ground. When I wound the watch, I thought about how I wanted time to speed up to bring Dad home, and I wanted time to slow down so Tem could be my best friend longer.

It was five in the morning in Turkey. Dad would still be sleeping. I wrapped the watch in a bandanna and set it on my nightstand. I heard it ticking. I heard the wind blowing. Winter was coming, my last winter with Tem.

Chapter Six

For Halloween Tem and I trick-or-treated as a picnic. I wore a red-checked plastic tablecloth with a hole cut out for my head to go through. Tem carried an empty fried-chicken bucket and her ant farm. I don't think a lot of people got it, though, because Mom made me wear a jacket.

Afterward I spread all my treats out on Tem's family-room floor. I alphabetized my candy, the way I did every year—Almond Joy, Baby Ruth, Clark Bar, all the way to Zagnut. Tem just sat and ate hers out of the fried-chicken bucket.

Soccer season was winding down. At soccer games I missed Dad so badly, it hurt. He was practically the team cheerleader, pacing up and down the sidelines hollering "Shoot!" or "Pull the trigger!" whenever someone on our team had the ball. Without him there was such an empty, aching space.

I talked Mom and Tem into coming to the last game of the season. It wasn't like having Dad there. They sat huddled in blankets the whole time, never leaving their lawn chairs. I didn't blame them. It was freezing—you could see your breath. Why they didn't cancel the game was beyond me, but my cold nose and feet were nothing compared to my colossal humiliation.

In the third quarter Coach Judy put me in at back defender. I was standing right where I was supposed to be, down by our goal, when the ball, the players, the noise, everything, started rushing toward me.

"Go, Emma," Tem shouted from the sideline. I turned to give her a thumbs-up sign. After all, I didn't get many cheers on the soccer field.

Bang! Before I knew it, I felt a terrible blow to my backside. Suddenly everybody was going crazy. Some stupid girl on the other team had managed to land a good hard shot right on my butt. And that's only half of it. The ball had been headed out of bounds, but my rear end was sticking out at exactly the right angle. The ball bounced off me and into the goal! What are the odds of that happening?

Thanks to me and my contribution, the other team took the lead, three to two.

"Don't you dare laugh," I told Tem after the game, as I ran toward the car and she tried to keep up. "Now I'm the worst player on the team."

"If you hate soccer so much," said Tem, panting, "why don't you quit?"

"I don't know," I said, slowing down. "I guess because I've always played."

"Just because you've always done things one way doesn't mean you can't change," said Tem.

"I've thought about trying to quit soccer," I admitted, "but I don't like it when stuff changes. I like things to stay the same."

"But sometimes things have to change," said Tem.

We kept talking like that, about soccer, but we both knew it wasn't soccer we were really talking about.

November in Illinois is brown and dull. Tem and I spent a lot of time in my room—me drawing and Tem switching radio stations so she could sing along.

We hardly ever talked about her moving, so it didn't seem real—at least not real the way a social studies test on Wednesday is real. It was more of a darkness, like when you were a little kid and you knew something horrible lived under your bed and it was better not to look. We went on pretending all through November and into December, when even the sunlight was cold and darkness came early.

"What do you want for dinner?" Mom asked one afternoon, when a light snow was falling. She was lying on the couch in the family room with newspapers and magazines all around her. Newspapers belonged in the recycle stack in the utility room. Magazines belonged in the big green basket by the fireplace. I was tired of picking up. Mom's hair looked dirty, and she hadn't pulled it back. I washed my hair in the bathtub every night, twice.

"Can we have a real meal?" I asked. "Like lasagna and garlic bread and a salad?"

Mom let out a huge yawn. "It's so hard to cook for just two. I was thinking we'd order in Chinese."

Mom ate her cashew chicken out of the white box on the couch. I ate my sweet-and-sour pork at the table, off a plate. I had set my place at the table carefully, with a napkin folded in half underneath my white plastic fork. We always fold napkins in half.

"Is Dad coming home for Christmas?" I asked Mom, but I knew the answer.

"No, Emma, it's just too far."

"Are we decorating the house?"

"I guess we could," said Mom, yawning. "If you want to."

"I want a tree," I said. "It doesn't have to be big, but let's get a little one and put it in the corner of the family room the way we always do. And I want the red light-up bells around the front door, same as always, and the manger scene on the piano."

"What about gifts?" asked Mom. "What do you want for your big present this year?"

I'd thought about that.

"In-line skates," I said.

"In-line skates? Aren't you kind of young? Would you be able to use them?"

I stood up and threw my napkin on the table. I scooted my chair up so hard that it knocked my glass over.

"Meaghan VanHook is getting in-line skates," I shouted. "She's getting in-line skates, her father is home, and her mother already has their house decorated for Christmas. Meaghan's the nastiest person I know, and she has everything I want."

I could see the tears in Mom's eyes. I guess I'd meant to put them there, but I hated seeing those tears.

"Of course," I said in a joking voice, trying to make things better, "Meaghan's house is all done in burgundy and evergreen. Red and green aren't fancy enough for them."

Mom smiled, but it wasn't the real kind of smile where your teeth show. She curled back up on the couch and pulled the granny-square afghan around her. She picked up the *TV Guide* and started thumbing through it. I tried to remember what her real smile looked like.

Chapter Seven

Dad called that night, late. It wasn't a Sunday. It was like he knew we were falling apart. Mom got me out of bed to talk to him. She went into the kitchen to make coffee.

"I'm worried about my girls," Dad said. "Try to be happy, Emma. Let's all make the best of this."

"How much longer, Dad?" I asked. "It's already the middle of December. You've been away sixty-three days."

"Three or four months," said Dad.

I was tired of asking questions when I already knew the answers. There was lots of static, like ghosts haunting the phone lines across the world.

"Dad," I whispered, "I can't really count on Mom."

"Can't hear you, Emma," said Dad. "Speak up."

"Never mind," I said.

I heard Mom talking to Dad on the phone for a long time after I went back to bed. I got Dad's watch out. I hadn't been winding it. The time was all wrong, but I wound it anyway and put it under my pillow. I could hear the ticking as I went to sleep, and Mom's voice drifting down the hall.

The next day, when I got home from school, the red light-up bells were on the door. The manger scene was on the piano, and a tree—a big tree—stood in the corner of the family room.

"Mom, what on earth—"

"Emma," Mom interrupted, "I hope you don't have a lot of homework. I was thinking you and I could decorate the tree right now. Then, I was thinking, maybe you'd like to call Tem and invite her for dinner. I've got a pan of lasagna in the oven. After dinner, I was thinking that the three of us could cut out paper snowflakes to hang in the windows."

Mom sure was doing a lot of thinking. Her blue eyes were bright as Christmas lights, and she sounded as if she had laughter inside that spilled over into her voice. Maybe things were going to get better. I said yes to all of it.

Tem gave up early on the snowflakes. Her snowflakes all came out like blobs with holes in them. We put Christmas music on, and Tem sang along with every carol. Tem could really sing, even the high notes in "O Holy Night." We sat there, the three of us at the table, Mom and I cutting snowflakes and Tem singing and all three of us drinking hot chocolate from mugs with peppermint stirring sticks.

It had been a long time since I had felt like this, all put together inside. I wanted to draw a picture of the three of us sitting there, warm and happy, the kitchen light soft around us and the music bright as peppermint.

Why was Mom so much happier all of a sudden? I wondered what Dad had said to her on the phone. I wondered about that all the way up to December twenty-fifth.

For the first Christmas in my life the sun was up before I was. I guess without Dad home I knew, even in my sleep, that I wasn't in much of a hurry.

Nearly all my packages were clothes, as usual. One box held different-colored barrettes to hold my bangs back. They had grown below my eyes.

Mom couldn't wait for me to open my big present. I knew by the flat box that it wasn't in-line skates. I was secretly glad. Mom was probably right about the skates—they'd be too hard to use, and I would fall and break a couple of important bones.

"Come on, open it," Mom said.

There it was, her real smile.

I peeled off the paper slowly, to make it last. I lifted the lid. Dozens of markers lay inside. The grownup, art-store kind of markers that stain your clothes and smell dangerous and cost a lot of money. The colors were beautiful: scarlet lake, peacock, grape, parrot green. Each marker had a tip on either end, one wide and one skinny. Best of all, there were three flesh colors, so I could color me the right color and Tem the right color and we both didn't have to be orange.

"Thanks," I said. "I mean it. It's a perfect present. Thanks."

"I talked it over with Dad. We came up with the idea together," Mom said, watching me line them up, color by color, in rainbow order. "I'm glad you're pleased."

"I am," I said. And I was.

It was strange not to have Dad there in his recliner, trying a new tie on over his pajamas. A couple of times I looked over at his chair, as if the looking would make him appear.

Tem came over before lunch. I gave her a new CD, *Best of Broadway.* I had designed the wrapping paper myself, with my old markers— yellow stars, red Christmas-tree balls, and green pine trees.

Tem gave us a pair of those friendship necklaces where each person wears half a heart that is broken in a jagged line down the middle. If you put the two pieces together, the heart was complete and it read *Best Friends*. It was supposed to show two halves of the same friendship, but all I could see was half a broken heart hanging around each of our necks.

I spent the afternoon coloring a Christmas picture for Dad. The house was quiet. I drew the Christmas tree with Mom standing next to it and me at the coffee table coloring the Christmas picture that I was actually coloring.

When I finished, I realized the picture I had drawn had leaked through to the page below, making a shadow picture. I looked at it for a long time and decided to send Dad the shadow picture instead of the real one. It was a shadow Christmas, not quite the real thing, because he wasn't there.

After dinner I had a sudden thought.

"Wait a minute," I said. "Why didn't Dad send you a present?"

"It's a little complicated," Mom said, reaching for my hand across the table. "I've been waiting since Dad called the other night to tell you this. I'm really excited about something, and I hope you'll be okay with it."

What was she talking about?

"I'm getting *two* big presents for Christmas this year," Mom went on, "but neither one is the kind you can wrap in a box. Number one, I'm going back to school—to Parkland Junior College for a computer course. It's time I learned some new skills. I'm planning to go back to work eventually."

"That's great, Mom," I said. "I've wanted you to do that for a long time—you know that."

"I know you have," said Mom, looking thoughtful. Her face brightened.

"And part two," she said, "is that I'm going to fly over and visit Dad for five weeks."

"What?" I said. This couldn't be happening. "What are you saying? First I find out Tem's leaving, then Dad leaves, and now you're leaving me too?"

"Of course not. Don't be silly. Dad didn't leave you. He's overseas finishing a project. I'm not leaving you either. I'm just going over for a visit, that's all."

I stared at her. For the life of me I couldn't see the difference.

"Oh, Emma," Mom said. "I guess I can understand why you're feeling a little left behind. But the time will go by quickly, you'll see, and before you know it, I'll be back and then Dad will be back and we'll all be together again."

I didn't say anything.

"Please don't be mad at me," said Mom. "It makes everything harder for both of us."

"I'm happy you're going back to school, Mom. It's the other part, the leaving me part." My voice was quiet, a shadow of a voice. "Can't I come too?"

"No, honey," Mom said. "You know you couldn't miss that much school. But don't worry—I'm not leaving until January twenty-third. That's almost a month away. I've already spoken with Great-Aunt Grace. She said she'd be delighted to come down from Chicago and stay with you."

I had no words. The incredibly bad news had just gotten ten times worse. Great-Aunt Grace rode the train down for dinner sometimes. She hardly talked at all, and when she did, it was about these weird organ concerts that she used to go around giving. I heard a tape of one once. The music she played sounded exactly like those old monster movies when the lights in the castle go out, and the thunder crashes all around, and someone is about to be killed.

I couldn't imagine how I'd get through this. I couldn't even think a thought straight through. With Great-Aunt Grace in charge, I'd be the only one left who knew how things should be done and when I was supposed to be where. And what if I got scared about something? Then what?

"I love you, Emma," said Mom.

"Don't say that," I said. "Those are just words. Anybody can say words. You can't count on words. Words don't keep things running the way they're supposed to. Words aren't there in the middle of the night."

"I do love you, though," Mom said.

"Then don't go," I said.

Mom came around the table and touched my shoulder. Her touch was as soft as a whisper.

"I can see this is a little difficult for you," she said, "but believe me, someday when you're a grownup, you'll understand."

I had my first clear thought of the evening. I knew, beyond a shadow of a doubt, that if I lived to be a hundred and ten, I would never, ever understand.

Chapter Eight

The day after Christmas was cold and cloudy. The wind picked the snowflakes up off the ground and blew them around, not content to let anything stay put.

Mom fixed oatmeal for breakfast, the kind out of the round box.

"Mom," I said, "it's terrible enough that you're leaving me for five weeks. But . . . Great-Aunt Grace? Couldn't I at least stay with Tem?"

I put five giant spoonfuls of brown sugar on my oatmeal. I knew I could get away with it.

"No, honey," said Mom. "Not for five weeks. That's too long."

"Not too long for you to leave me," I pointed out.

"Aunt Grace used to stay with me when I

was little. She'll be a lovely companion for you."

A lovely companion? What on earth was a *lovely companion?* Someone who was shriveled up and played creepy music? Someone who didn't know how to make a grilled cheese crunchy on the outside and oozing on the inside? Someone who didn't know that after a nightmare I like milk and plain crackers and not a lot of questions?

I sat there at the table with my oatmeal getting cold and looked at Mom. She was smiling a goofy smile, sure that everything would work out just fine. I knew that I should feel happy for her. I knew that I should feel excited that she was going to see Dad. But I also knew that how you should feel and how you really felt could be miles apart, as many miles as it was from that kitchen table to Turkey.

I wasn't hungry. My oatmeal was dark brown from all that sugar. And cold. I started to put my coat on to go to Tem's.

"Listen, Emma," Mom began.

"No, stop," I said. "If you're going off for five weeks, I can't stop you. But don't expect me to sit here and act like I'm happy about it. And another thing: I don't want to hear any crap about how wonderful creepy old Great-Aunt Grace is."

"Okay," Mom said and smiled.

Had she heard a word I said?

I headed over to Tem's. There was a new sign in their yard, a FOR SALE sign, with the name of some lady on it and a phone number people could call and hear a recording listing all the details about the house, Tem's house, the house that had always seemed part mine.

Tem and I curled up on either end of her living-room couch, sharing the afghan across our legs, which met in the middle.

"My mom is abandoning me too," I told her.

"What do you mean?" asked Tem.

"She's leaving January twenty-third to go stay with my dad in Turkey. She says she's 'only' going to be gone for five weeks, but actually she's skipping out for the entire month of February and won't be back until the beginning of March."

"February is a short month," Tem pointed out.

I glared at her.

"Sorry," said Tem. "It stinks, Emma, it really does."

She tucked the afghan around my feet, shuffled out to the kitchen, and came back with a new roll of Life Savers. We started working our way through it. Tem gave me every single cherry and orange, so I could tell she felt bad for me.

"At least *you'll* be here," I said to Tem.

"Yeah," said Tem. "At least I'll be here."

"I saw that stupid sign out front," I said. "I

don't want to think about somebody else living in your house."

Tem sighed. "Mom says we've *got* to sell the house or the deal is off. The junior college isn't paying for our move."

I sat up. "Say that again, Tem."

"I said, Mom says we've got to sell the house or the deal is off. The junior—"

"Stop!" I cried. "Does this say anything to you?"

Tem was starting to smile.

"If we can stop the sale . . ." I said.

"We won't have to move!" Tem shouted triumphantly.

Tem got a pad of paper and a pencil and handed it to me. I stretched out on the living-room floor. *Top Ten Ways to Stop the Sale of a House,* I wrote at the top.

"Ideas?" I asked Tem.

"What if the house smelled real bad?" she asked.

"Excellent," I said. "We can find a dead squirrel or something on the road. We'll wrap it in foil and keep it in the freezer. When we know someone is coming to look at your house, we'll thaw it out in the microwave and put it in the hall closet. A dead squirrel could really stink things up!"

"Cool," said Tem.

I wrote "Dead squirrel or something" on the list.

"What if the lawn was three feet high next spring?" asked Tem.

I looked out the window at the snow-covered yard, the neatly shoveled sidewalk.

"Tem," I said, "your dad keeps the yard looking perfect."

Tem smiled. "But suppose I poured a can of pop in the gas tank of the lawn mower? You can't mow without a lawn mower. My mom says pop rots out the inside of anything."

"Good idea," I said. "Number two, 'Trash the lawn mower before spring.'"

We thought for a while.

"I've got it," I said. "What if people think the neighborhood is full of weirdoes? Suppose they've got little kids—they'd be picky about a thing like that."

"Like what?" asked Tem.

"Like if I dressed really strange and every time someone came to look at your house, I was out front, singing loud, and turning cartwheels, and making faces."

"They'd just think you were a goofy kid," said Tem.

"Yeah," I said. "A goofy kid they don't want their kid to turn out like."

"Good point," said Tem.

We spent the rest of the day adding to our list.

We made another list of research questions—like How do you get to the tap water before it comes out of the faucet? and How do you operate that flap inside the fireplace?

"Mrs. Beauman would be proud of our organizational skills," I said to Tem.

"You betcha," said Tem.

January crawled along like a frozen snail, headed toward Mom's departure. I kept reminding myself to treasure my time with Tem, but it's hard to have fun when you keep telling yourself you'd better hurry up and enjoy someone before they disappear.

Several days before Mom was to leave, Great-Aunt Grace came down on the train. Great-Aunt Grace had these incredibly droopy eyelids. She had to tilt her head back to see you. She walked in soft, creepy mouse steps with her hands clutched, like bird claws, across her bony chest.

"You two are going to get along great," Mom said for the fifteenth time.

Great-Aunt Grace tipped her head back and looked at me with the small available part of her eyeballs. She looked as excited about the prospect of our spending five weeks together as I was.

Great-Aunt Grace said nothing.

I said nothing.

"Well, then," Mom chirped along, "take a look at what I bought today."

She showed us a suitcase with little hidden wheels.

Great-Aunt Grace had nothing to say about that suitcase, and neither did I.

"And Emma," said Mom, "I have a wonderful surprise for you."

She pulled out a big box.

"A pair of in-line skates, just your size."

Great-Aunt Grace said nothing, but I found plenty to say.

"That stinks!" I shouted. "Presents for Christmas and birthdays are great, but a big present because you're going away is just plain stupid. And besides, it's the middle of winter. I couldn't go skating if I wanted to. If you think it makes up for leaving me, you're wrong."

Mom quit smiling. She pushed her lips together, hard. Great-Aunt Grace tipped her head back and her face didn't change one bit. I could tell my terrible, horrible behavior came as no particular surprise to her.

Chapter Nine

For three days it was Great-Aunt Grace, Mom, and me. We were all tiptoeing around each other with lots of *please*s and *thank-you*s and *excuse-me*s. No one said anything trickier than "It's snowing outside" or "Please pass the biscuits, thank you." I figured no one wanted another blowup from me. Twice, though, when I walked in after school, I heard Mom and Great-Aunt Grace at the kitchen table laughing. Laughing! I couldn't imagine what Great-Aunt Grace would ever find to laugh about.

I felt bad about the skate incident. I slipped a card that I'd drawn with my new markers inside Mom's suitcase. It said "Bon Voyage and Don't Forget Me" in blush pink on a periwinkle background.

I tried to be nice to Mom the night before she left.

"Tell Dad I said hi," I told her. "Tell him there are things about him I can't remember anymore, like how his fingernails look."

"Hang in there," said Mom. "I'll be back in five short weeks."

Five short weeks. Five short weeks with Great-Aunt Grace. Mrs. Beauman had a name for words you put together that are opposites. I hadn't bothered to learn it. Who would have guessed a word like that ever would fit into my life?

A taxi came and Mom turned to me. We looked at each other, but not the kind of looking where your eyes hook up.

"Bye, Mom," I said.

"I'll miss you, Emma," Mom said.

She turned and walked outside, and when she pulled the door shut, it closed with a soft click that echoed through the house.

Great-Aunt Grace cleared her throat.

"There's a National Geographic special on television," she said.

"Fine," I said.

It was our longest conversation of the evening. It may have been our longest conversation of the week.

Great-Aunt Grace knew how to cook one thing and only one thing. Sausage.

She fixed smoked sausage links and fried apples, sausage patties and pancakes, and crumbled-up sausage in biscuits that came rolled in a can. Then she started all over again at the top of the list with smoked links and fried apples. At any rate, I liked knowing what to expect.

At lunch Tem pointed out that I was actually eating hot lunches. Usually I only nibbled at a few things on my tray, like dessert. But with Great-Aunt Grace in charge, I figured it might be a good idea to eat up when I had the chance. Any day I could suddenly get sick of sausage dinners, and I was pretty sure Great-Aunt Grace didn't have a backup menu plan.

"Are you trying out for the school play?" Tem asked, offering me her peaches.

Northpoint Elementary was putting on *Joseph and the Amazing Technicolor Dreamcoat* February twenty-sixth and twenty-seventh. Everybody was all wound up about it. The walls of the cafeteria were plastered with sign-up sheets. *Joseph* music was even being played over the loudspeaker, as if anybody could hear it over the noise in the cafeteria.

"*Joseph* is a musical," I said, eating Tem's potato logs. "Small problem: I can't sing."

"I want the lead part of the narrator more than I've ever wanted anything," said Tem.

"I'm not surprised," I said. "Since you're going to be a Broadway star, this is a good first step." I grabbed the peanut butter and celery sticks she'd left on her tray.

"I'm trying for the lead too," said Meaghan VanHook from across the table, as if we'd been talking to her. "Don't count on beating me out. I've been taking private voice lessons for two months getting ready for the audition."

And just to prove her point, Meaghan started singing these quivery warble sounds, all with an "ah-ah-ah" sound instead of words.

"Gosh," said Tem. I knew what she was thinking.

"Oh, cool it, Meaghan," I said. "I'll admit you can sing. Just like the old ladies in the church choir. But that doesn't mean you'll get the part." I said this like I actually knew something about theater auditions, which I did not.

"Oh, yeah?" said Meaghan, inspecting her shiny, pearl-white fingernails. "My mom says I have that special something."

"And who'd argue with her mom?" I whispered to Tem.

"No whispering," shouted Meaghan, "or I'll tell."

"Well, then," I said, speaking right up, "did it ever occur to you that you might *not* get the lead?"

"Yes," said Meaghan. "If that happens, then I should definitely get the part of Potiphar's wife."

"Who's Potiphar's wife?" I asked.

"She's rich and evil," said Meaghan. "And it's

still a leading role. If I get that part, my mom says she'll make me a beautiful costume."

"Sounds like a good part for you," I said.

The bell rang before she had a chance to respond.

Walking back to class with Tem, I said, "You know what's the worst thing about Meaghan VanHook?"

"The fact that she pays to have her fingernails done?" asked Tem.

"No," I said. "I bet that's all her mom's idea. No, the worst thing about Meaghan is the way I am around her. She turns me into this mean, scratchy person."

"Don't worry about it," said Tem.

"Tem," I said, "I never ever feel that way around you. I wish there was something I could do as well as you can sing. Good luck. You'd better get the lead."

"Thanks," said Tem.

I crossed my fingers and wished. I also prayed and stepped on no cracks all the way back to class.

Tem said she thought she sang pretty well in the audition but that Meaghan did a good job too. It was two days before the cast list was posted. The waiting was awful. When I saw the list, printed out on sheets of green paper and taped to the school office door, I was almost afraid to look.

My heart was beating a mile a minute as I walked up, and bang!—there it was! Tem got the lead role of the narrator.

"Yes!" I shouted, pumping my fist in the air.

Meaghan VanHook would be appearing as Potiphar's wife, the beautiful but evil one. Everything made sense. It happened as it should have. I guess I got a little carried away by all that, because I marched right into the cafeteria and signed up to paint sets.

I'd never done a cocurricular activity before. I'd always gone straight home after school and either played with Tem or worked on an art project until dinner. This was a huge change in my routine, not that Great-Aunt Grace would know any better. But there I was, signed up to work on sets every day from three o'clock to six o'clock. I was part of the technical crew. The kids in the cast called us "techies," a name I sort of liked.

Mr. Freeman, the art teacher, was in charge. He was tall and wore jeans and denim shirts, and ties that looked like the comics.

The day after I signed up, all ten of us set designers met on the empty stage after school. Nobody I knew very well was there, and I wished like crazy that Tem was sitting next to me. Mr. Freeman showed us sketches of what the set was going to look like. Everybody was shouting out ideas, but

I just sat there, and nobody asked for my opinion about anything.

Mr. Freeman assigned me to work with the Taylor twins the first couple of days, until I learned my way around. Ashley and Christine Taylor were in sixth grade, and they'd worked on the previous year's show.

At first I thought Ashley and Christine looked exactly alike. I started telling one of them the long, involved plot of a movie I'd seen. I was sure I was talking to Ashley, so I even said her name a couple of times, the way you do when you're in the middle of a conversation with someone. When I finished relating the plot, she smiled and said, "That sounds like a good movie. By the way, I'm Christine."

I felt so stupid, but she laughed and said not to worry about it.

After a couple of days I didn't have a bit of trouble telling them apart. They both had reddish-blond hair, and probably a trillion freckles between them. Christine, however, had a more pointy nose, and Ashley blinked all the time. But it was more than that. In a lot of ways they were as different as Tem and me, once you got to know them. Maybe that was why they got along so well with each other.

"Hey, you," Ashley said on one of those first days, "hold this support board while I nail it."

I held the piece of wood the way she showed

me. We were building flats, which are huge framed surfaces that can be painted to look like houses or pyramids or palm trees. I'd never nailed anything in my life, but Ashley was charging around with a hammer stuck in her belt and a pocket full of nails as if she had an after-school job on a construction site.

She started singing crazy songs and pounding nails in rhythm. "La, la, bamba" . . . bang, bang . . . "la, la, bamba" . . . bang, bang . . . "ya, ya, ya, ya."

It was amazing. We got in sync, and before I knew it, the whole flat was nailed together.

"Good job," Ashley said to me. "What's your name?"

"Emma," I said.

"Next time, Emma," said Ashley, "sing along."

That was Ashley. Loud and bossy, but in a way that made you want to do what she said.

Christine loved to paint little tiny perfect details. I think she liked to go off in her own little world while she was painting, and I knew how that felt.

"It's fun to paint for a long time," I said to her one day. "You can kind of get lost in it." Immediately, I realized how dumb that sounded.

"Oh, yes!" Christine answered. "I'd rather paint than eat, or sleep, or go to school. For sure I'd rather paint than go to school."

"Ever work with markers?" I asked.

"All the time!" said Christine, and that was it. We talked for an hour about all the art projects we'd done and all the ones we wanted to do.

The crew divided itself into small groups. A couple of the boys worked on lights, and two girls worked on signs and props. Some of the kids took on the project of building and painting the pyramid for Act Two. Their jeans were so covered with paint from the pyramid, they looked like gray jeans instead of blue jeans.

There was a buzzing sort of excitement building all over the school because of the show. The school days seemed to fly by, probably because I spent a lot of class time thinking about the sets. By three o'clock each day I couldn't wait to get backstage.

Sometimes all of us on the crew talked while we worked. Sometimes we didn't, but it was the working-together kind of quiet that felt as though we were still talking.

One day Mr. Freeman suggested I work on painting the packs on the camels that belonged to the hairy Ishmaelites. We worked backstage. It was big and dusty and smelled of paint and freshly cut wood. The chorus was rehearsing out in the "house," which means the seats where the audience would sit. Ribbons of the songs they were rehearsing floated over the heavy velvet curtains.

I realized Mr. Freeman had stopped spray-painting stairs and was watching me work.

"You're good at this, Emma," he said. "You have artistic talent."

"Thanks," I whispered, continuing to paint. Inside, I was full of warm honey.

Artistic talent—he says I have artistic talent. I kept saying it to myself over and over, my paintbrush gliding across the cardboard in bright, clear strokes.

When we were done for the day, Ashley, Christine, and I went into the backstage storage room to put stuff away. It was full of props from long-ago plays. We pulled out dusty chairs, tables, and lamps and made a pretend living room.

"I'm hungry," I said. "Maybe we should have invented a kitchen."

Ashley stuck a pipe in her mouth and sat down on a dusty stuffed chair.

"Do tell," she said in a deep voice. "Whatever might we be dining upon tonight?"

Christine threw a maid's apron around her neck. She picked up a flower pot and pretended to stir it with a cane.

"Oh, my most darling one," she said, batting

her eyelashes up and down, "I'm serving stewed possum and fried corn flakes."

"How simply lovely," said Ashley, and she picked up a cow bell and rang it.

I put on an Abraham Lincoln hat and walked over to her in stiff butler steps.

"You rang?" I said in my deepest voice.

At that very moment the school bell, which rang every hour whether school was in session or not, began to ring. I jumped a foot, and then we laughed and laughed. We finally got quiet, and I said, "You rang?" again, and the laughing started all over.

Walking home, I decided to write *butler* in my journal so I'd remember to tell Dad about our good time. I thought about all the fun I was having with Ashley and Christine. It was the kind of fun you wanted to tell somebody about. Like Tem. I always told her everything, but I was being pretty quiet about this.

What would Tem think? I'd done all those silly things with somebody else. Would she think I'd forgotten her already? And what about Tem? Was she making new friends during rehearsals?

Chapter Ten

Great-Aunt Grace and I had settled into a quiet, comfortable routine. She would wait to start dinner until I got home. We'd eat a quiet sausage dinner, which, to my surprise, tasted good, night after night. Then I'd do my homework and get ready for the next day. Great-Aunt Grace was trying hard, I could tell. She did laundry every day, and she even ironed my pajamas.

When I got home that day, I sat at the kitchen table as Great-Aunt Grace got ready to cook smoked sausage links.

"Mr. Freeman says I have artistic talent," I told her.

"I've been looking at your drawings on the refrigerator," said Great-Aunt Grace. "I think Mr.

Freeman is right. It's the same as in music. Some people can simply pull more out of themselves. That's called talent."

I was surprised Great-Aunt Grace could talk this much.

"Were you talented at playing the organ?" I asked.

"I guess so," said Great-Aunt Grace. "And it led me into a lot of interesting experiences. But I wonder, Emma, if maybe you don't wish I'd spent more of my time learning to cook."

"I'm cool with the sausage dinners," I told her.

"Oh, I'm relieved," said Great-Aunt Grace. "Tell me more about your set-building."

Great-Aunt Grace sat down at the kitchen table opposite me, holding the package of sausage links.

I started telling her about the sets, and Ashley and Christine, and the story of Joseph. Pretty soon I was telling her about Tem and how she had the lead and how she was my best friend and she was moving away in the summer, which would pretty much ruin my life.

Great-Aunt Grace listened. She acted as if everything I said was important, and when she didn't understand what I meant, she'd ask questions until she did. They weren't the kind of questions that were supposed to make me think something, like Don't you think you'll make a new best friend?

or Don't you think you should try to adjust? They were the kind of questions that meant she wanted to know the answer: "How do you paint a flat?" "Why do you like Tem so much?" "How do you feel about your folks being gone so long?"

I told her I didn't like change. I wanted people to stay put. I told her I didn't like being left. First by Dad, then by Mom, and most of all by Tem.

"What are you afraid of?" Great-Aunt Grace asked.

Suddenly, that seemed like the biggest question in the world. It filled me up with its awful, sad bigness. I opened my mouth, but no words came out, only whimpering. Crying, really.

I expected Great-Aunt Grace to come running around the table and say, "There, there," or something like that, but she didn't. She sat in the chair opposite me and looked at me as though blubbering away at the kitchen table was a normal thing to do.

"I'm afraid of being left," I said, sniffling. "I'm afraid of being alone. It's okay when I'm busy, like working on the sets or talking on the phone to Tem. But at nights, sometimes, I feel so alone. I can hardly breathe, and I wonder who I am and how time goes on forever and if I'll feel alone even after I die. And if that feeling will go on forever and ever. And I don't know who I am or what I am or why I'm here—and I just want to hold on to Mom or Dad or Tem, only I can't count on them to be here. And besides all that, Tem's my forever best friend, and you only get one of those."

Great-Aunt Grace didn't say a word. She just nodded her head as though she thought the very same thoughts, which, of course, wasn't very likely.

"Tem and I had our whole lives worked out— her and me. We figured we'd marry best friends and live next door to each other, or at least in the same subdivision, and find jobs close by and have kids at the same time. It was all settled."

"Yes, I can see that," said Great-Aunt Grace.

"And then there's my parents," I said, sniffling and wiping the remaining tears off my face with the sleeve of my sweatshirt.

"Just so," said Great-Aunt Grace. "There's your parents."

"Well, some kids have dads who *never* have to travel for their work. They come home every day at the same time."

"That's true," said Great-Aunt Grace.

"Of course," I said in a stronger voice, "some kids in my class hardly ever see their dads at all, and I know one girl who wishes she *never* had to see her dad because he's mean and yells at her all the time."

"That's too bad," said Great-Aunt Grace.

"Yes, it is," I said. "And not fair. I'd love to see *my* dad. I miss him so much. I miss the way he makes things funny, and I miss the way the house feels safe when he's home."

"I'll bet you do," said Great-Aunt Grace.

"Some of the kids in my class don't know how lucky they have it," I said.

"Still, though," said Great-Aunt Grace, "we're talking about you."

Boy, were we ever. I was like a crazy person on a talk show, blabbing on and on.

"And then there's my mom . . ." I said, my thoughts trailing off in a hundred directions.

"Yes," said Great-Aunt Grace, softly, "you haven't said much about your mom."

It was funny, but I'd never noticed that underneath Great-Aunt Grace's droopy eyelids, her eyes were bright blue and sparkly.

"Well," I said, "I know I'm *supposed* to be happy that she got to go visit Dad. . . ."

I stopped. I was dead stuck on that thought.

"I don't think that would make *me* very happy if I were you," said Great-Aunt Grace.

"Well, it doesn't!" I said in a loud voice. I was practically shouting. "I think it's selfish. Sometimes Mom does just what she wants. If she feels like staying in bed all day with a headache or flying off to Turkey when I need her here—she just goes off and does it. My P.E. shoes are too small, and I'm supposed to come up with this family tree for social studies. Moms are supposed to be around for stuff like that, only mine isn't. *She's* in Turkey."

Now I'd done it. Mom was Great-Aunt Grace's only niece.

"I should imagine I'd feel very much the same way if I were you," said Great-Aunt Grace.

I looked closely to see if she was kidding, but Great-Aunt Grace wasn't much of a kidder.

Neither one of us said anything for a long time. I could hear the clock ticking in the hallway, the doves calling to each other in the yard. The street lamp burned yellow outside the kitchen window.

"I remember your mom when she was your age," said Great-Aunt Grace quietly, as if she was looking backward through time.

"You do?" I asked. This surprised me, although it shouldn't have. Mom never talked much about her childhood.

"She was like you in some ways," Great-Aunt Grace said. "She used to worry too."

"What did Mom have to worry about?" I asked.

"Money, for one thing," said Great-Aunt Grace. "Her dad, your grandfather, was out of work a lot. I recall that your mom had to earn her own money for clothes."

"She did?" I asked, surprised again. I got an allowance and had never had to earn my own money for anything. "How on earth did she earn money when she was a kid?"

"She baby-sat quite often, as I remember," said Great-Aunt Grace. "And she worked at a small store near her house—Cohen's Variety, I think it was called. It's gone now. Your mom started by cleaning and dusting after school and worked her way up to running the cash register."

"No kidding!" I said.

"That's where she met your dad. He came in for shoe polish. It's odd, I remember that. I even recall it was black shoe polish."

"That's not very romantic," I countered.

"Still," said Great-Aunt Grace, "he swept your mom right off her feet. He was older, and I think to your mom he seemed very stable."

"That's my dad," I said. "Steady as a rock."

"Your mom was barely out of high school when they got married," said Great-Aunt Grace.

"Wow," I said. All of this was news to me.

"And you came along right away," said Great-Aunt Grace. She smiled. "We were all pretty excited when you came along."

"Is that why Mom didn't go to college?" I asked. "Because of me?"

"Partly you and partly the money," said

Great-Aunt Grace. "Your mom needed to work so your dad could finish engineering school."

"Do you think Mom's nervous about going back to school now?" I asked.

"Maybe," said Great-Aunt Grace. "What do you think?"

"Maybe," I said.

"I wonder if Mom gets kind of scared when Dad's gone," I said.

"Could be," said Great-Aunt Grace.

We were both quiet for a while. I had a lot to think about.

"Emma," Great-Aunt Grace said, "sometimes when I played the organ, I'd shut my eyes and quit thinking, and the notes would come just right."

"Huh?" I said.

What did playing the organ have to do with anything? If this was advice, and it seemed like advice, it didn't make any sense.

"I've got an awful lot of faith in you," she said, scooting her chair back from the table.

"You do?" I said.

"Sometimes you just have to play the notes on the page, but how you play them is up to you."

"Okay, sure," I said doubtfully, still thinking about Mom.

Great-Aunt Grace stood up. I guessed our talk was over. She took the sausages out of the package and leaned against the stove. She opened her mouth to say something, but instead let out the most horrible, strangled-sounding cry.

"I've burned my hand," she said, holding it up in front of her.

I ran over and looked at her hand. She must have put it on the hot stove burner. Already there were clear round rings of blisters.

I burned my finger once on a cookie sheet. Even that tiny burn hurt so much that I cried.

"Run it under cold water," I said, guiding Great-Aunt Grace to the sink. Her blouse was all sweaty.

"Keep your hand up in the air so the blood won't run into it," I said after a few minutes, trying to think of everything Mom or Dad would do.

"I'm not sure I can fix supper," said Great-Aunt Grace. Her voice sounded shaky.

"Supper?" I said. "You nearly burned your hand off and you're worried about supper?"

"A growing girl like you needs a good meal," she said. She looked very old and very breakable, like one of the dolls from my foreign-doll collection that you're not supposed to play with.

"Great-Aunt Grace," I said in a voice that sounded for all the world like Mrs. Beauman's, "I tell you what we're going to do. We're going to order a pizza."

"Order a pizza?" said Great-Aunt Grace, as astonished as if I'd said we were flying to Ethiopia for dinner.

"Yep," I said. "A pizza."

"What kind of pizza?" asked Great-Aunt Grace.

"Well, let me think," I said as I looked up the number for Domino's.

"Yes, what types of pizza do they have?" she asked.

I looked at her, with her hand up in the air. "Oh my gosh," I said. "How dumb of me. We're getting a medium pizza, thin crust . . . sausage. Extra sausage."

Chapter Eleven

Time was flying by. We were already up to the final week before the show—Tech Week, they called it. We had one set left to paint. It was the twenty-second of February. Ashley, Christine, and I worked late after the others had left. Mr. Freeman brought back tacos. We sat on the stage and used the wrappers for plates. Mr. Freeman picked out his lettuce too.

"Mr. Freeman," said Ashley, biting into a taco, "you know what we ought to do? We ought to have an art club here at school."

"We could paint a mural on the wall by the front door," added Christine.

I could tell they'd been thinking about this.

"I think that's an excellent idea," said Mr. Freeman. "An art club would be a lot of fun."

Maybe he'd been thinking about an art club too.

"You'd join, wouldn't you, Emma?" Mr. Freeman asked.

"Yeah, come on, Emma," said Ashley and Christine at exactly the same time.

I nodded. "Sure," I said. "An art club sounds great."

My mind was spinning. I'd never figured I'd be part of anything that had a picture in the yearbook. The only organized thing I'd ever done besides school was soccer, which, number one, I hated, and number two, I was terrible at. An art club would be perfect for me. Maybe I could even quit soccer and just do art.

"Could we take field trips?" I asked.

"Good thinking," said Mr. Freeman. "We could visit the Krannert Art Museum for starters."

"Hey, Emma," said Ashley, "very cool idea."

"Thanks," I said. "And thanks for the tacos, Mr. Freeman."

"No problem," he said. "You guys are my A team."

When we finished our tacos, Mr. Freeman crumpled his taco wrapper and wandered off to check lighting. Stage lights, I'd learned, get covered with colored transparent sheets called gels that can really change the way things look onstage.

Mr. Freeman hadn't been happy with the way the Egyptian scenes looked, so he started trying different combinations of gels. I was pleased he was so picky about how our sets looked in the lights. In the end he decided on amber lights that looked bright and hot, just the way it probably felt in Egypt.

"I love all this," I said, twirling around onstage in front of the Sphinx and the pyramid. "It's like playing pretend, or dress-up, but so much better."

"Sit down, Emma," said Christine. She scooted up behind me and began French braiding my hair. By now my bangs had grown down to my ears, and it drove Christine-the-neatnik crazy when they hung in my face.

"Ouch," I said. "That pulls."

"Oh, hush, Emma," Christine said. "I'm about to make you bee-*you*-tee-ful."

"Maybe we could have art club T-shirts," I said.

"Yeah," said Ashley, "but not T-shirts that look like everybody else's."

"We could use tie-dye," I said. "That would stick out."

"Yeah," said Christine, "and we could all wear them on days the club meets, so everyone will know."

"And eat their hearts out if they're not part of it," said Ashley.

We talked on and on about the art club while

Christine finished my hair and we put brushes, paints, and tools away.

The twins' mom gave me a ride home. Sitting in the back of their minivan, I thought about Tem. She got her worst grades in art. Would she feel left out? Should I just forget about joining an art club until next year, when Tem would be gone anyway?

When I got home, Great-Aunt Grace was in her shiny blue robe with bobby pins in her hair. Her hand was better now, just a couple of Band-Aids.

"Things go all right?" she asked.

"Oh, sure," I said. "Better than all right, actually. We're talking about starting an art club."

"You'd love that," said Great-Aunt Grace. "With your talent and the encouragement of friends, the sky's the limit for you." She paused, and a smile spread across her face like soft butter on toast.

"Maybe, Emma," she said, "I should just get your autograph now."

I laughed out loud and Great-Aunt Grace did too, a quiet coughing sort of laugh. I went over and kissed her papery, dry cheek.

"Just keep fixing me those great sausage dinners," I said. "I'll make you proud of me yet."

"I'm as proud as I can be right now," said Great-Aunt Grace, fiddling with her bathrobe button. She tipped her head back to get me in focus. "I always will be proud of you, Emma. You can count on that."

"Thanks," I said. How could I have been so wrong about her? "Tell you what, we'll count on each other."

"Well said," said Great-Aunt Grace.

That night, in bed, I wound Dad's gold watch and thought about him and Mom. I hoped Mom was doing okay in Turkey while Dad was at work all day.

I ran my fingers over the smooth cover. Time was ticking on. It was still a month or so before Dad came home, but Mom would be back in a week. I remembered when Mom left, and how I thought five weeks was forever. Actually, it had gone by pretty fast because of the play—the big, busy, magical play that had used up all my extra time. I didn't want *Joseph* ever to end.

The watch tumbled onto the bed as I suddenly realized something. If, for some reason, somebody had given me the chance to fly to Turkey at that exact moment, to be with Mom and Dad, I wouldn't have gone.

I wanted to be home for opening night. Of course, if someone was handing out choices, I'd want Mom and Dad home for opening night, too, not clear across the world in Turkey. When my big night was opening, it would already be the next day there.

I got out my *Day by Day* journal and a handful of markers. I wasn't writing in it much anymore. Dad and I always had okay conversations when he called, and I'd stopped thinking I had to write things down to discuss with him.

Now, instead of making lists of my activities, I was drawing sketches of what was going on around me. I'd drawn Great-Aunt Grace's hand with the rings of blisters, and I'd sketched our sets. I'd also tried to draw Ashley and Christine and Mr. Freeman, but I wasn't very good at faces.

On my bed, with the watch ticking, I decided to sketch some ideas for art club T-shirts. Maybe we could tie-dye the shirts and then have a logo silk-screened on top. I tried several designs. My favorite was a paintbrush with *Northpoint Art Club* written across the handle. I drew a green tie-dyed shirt with a purple paintbrush in the middle. It looked flat-out awesome.

That got me thinking. Maybe I could get a Saturday job at a T-shirt shop. It would be a reason to quit soccer. Probably I was too young, though, to get a real job. I'd have to keep thinking.

There had to be a way to do a lot more art and a lot less soccer.

Later, with the watch under my pillow, where its tick was muffled as a heartbeat, I dreamed Ashley, Christine, and I were painting a mural of pyramid shapes in primary colors.

Opening night finally arrived. Our call—which meant the time when we had to be at the theater—was six P.M. I had managed only two bites of pancake for supper.

I went backstage to the dressing room, which was actually the music room crammed full of costume racks and card tables weighed down with mirrors and makeup. The whole place was noisy with kids singing and shouting "Break a leg" back and forth across the tumble of flowers and helium balloons that said *Good Luck*.

Some girls from my class were doing makeup, drawing a black line across each dancer's eyelid and extending it out for an inch.

I found Tem and handed her three pink carnations in a milk-white vase that I'd bought at the grocery store.

"Thanks," said Tem.

"Ready?" I asked.

"Ready as I'll ever be," said Tem.

"Are you nervous?" I asked.

"A little," Tem said.

"You don't look it," I said.

Tem smiled. "That's because nerves are on the inside."

"Go get 'em, Tiger," I said. It was something we had always said to each other. "You'll be great."

Tem nodded at the next table over. Meaghan was sitting there among flowers and teddy bears and a whole bouquet of balloons.

She caught me looking.

"My mom got me a dozen roses," said Meaghan.

"That's nice," I said.

"Look," Meaghan went on, "they're long-stemmed."

"Who cares how tall flowers are?" I asked.

"Yeah, I know," said Meaghan. "Tall flowers won't keep me from messing up onstage."

"Are you nervous too?" asked Tem.

"I threw up," said Meaghan.

She did look sort of green. I grabbed some blush out of Meaghan's makeup bag and dabbed at her cheeks.

"You'll be fine," I said.

"Easy for you to say," said Meaghan. "You don't have to do anything."

"I already did my work," I said.

"Painting sets—big deal," said Meaghan. "The performers are the ones who really count."

"Yeah, right," I replied, wishing I hadn't bothered with the blush.

Meaghan stood up and walked over to the full-length mirror someone had propped up in the corner.

"How much does that costume weigh?" I asked, following her.

"A lot," said Meaghan.

Her costume, which her mother had made, consisted of a long, shiny purple dress covered with so many gold and silver sequins you could barely see any purple. Huge fake jewels were stuck here and there like Christmas-tree ornaments.

"If the lights are really bright, you might blind somebody," I said.

"My costume is totally awesome and you know it," said Meaghan. She was staring at herself in the mirror as if I wasn't even there. "In fact, I just might steal the show."

I left Meaghan looking in the mirror and pulled Tem behind the costume rack. "Listen, Tem," I whispered, "don't sing so well that people forget to notice my sets."

"Don't you worry," said Tem.

"Gotta go," I said. I think I was more nervous than Tem.

My name was printed in the program with the others under *Set Design*. I read it again and again. I was glad Great-Aunt Grace was in the audience. I wanted someone there who would be looking for my name first.

I paced back and forth backstage all through Act One. I worried about our sets, which was stupid. It wasn't like the paint was going to come peeling off. When I wasn't worrying, I felt proud. That was kind of stupid, too. I was only part of the crew, but I felt as though I'd built a movie set that was up for an Academy Award.

During intermission I went and found Great-Aunt Grace. She was still sitting in her seat, clutching her program.

"So, what do you think of the show?" I asked.

"The show?" asked Great-Aunt Grace. "Who can pay any attention to the show? I can't keep my eyes off the sets. They're beautiful."

"Thanks," I said, "thanks a lot." I paused, looking through my mind for words. "Great-Aunt Grace, I'm glad you're here. I mean I'm glad you came. I just wanted you to know that. I wish we hadn't taken so long to get to know each other."

"Well said." Great-Aunt Grace said that a lot. Smiling, she winked at me with one of her droopy old eyelids.

I sat down next to her to watch Act Two.

Joseph and the Amazing Technicolor Dreamcoat is the story of Joseph, who got sold into slavery by his brothers and exiled to Egypt, where he didn't know a single soul. Kind of like Tem being exiled by her parents to Kankakee, where she didn't know a single soul, instead of staying here where she belonged—with me.

Meaghan, as Potiphar's beautiful-but-evil wife, pranced onto the stage in all her jewels and sequins. She wiggled her hips like an Elvis impersonator. Her false eyelashes looked like spiders. I could tell she was really nervous when she first came onstage because I could hardly hear her. She got into it, though, and actually did a good job.

Tem sat on a stool in the corner of the stage. She had on khaki pants and a turtleneck. The spotlight hugged her with yellow light. When she sang, her voice filled up the air in the auditorium. It got warm and quiet, except for Tem's singing. Some people closed their eyes, but I was sure they weren't sleepy.

It seemed to me like the show was over in about ten minutes, but I knew it had lasted two hours.

The cast came onstage for curtain call. When Meaghan walked out, her mom jumped to her feet, and pretty soon everyone stood up and clapped. I'd heard the theater kids talk about this.

We were getting what they called a *standing o,* which was short for "standing ovation."

Tem walked on the stage last, with her hands in her pockets. The lights sparkled on her shiny black hair, and the audience clapped like thunder.

After the curtain call I asked Great-Aunt Grace to wait for me, and I went backstage to find Tem. She was with her parents. Tem's mom and dad were usually pretty quiet, but tonight they were full of smiles and compliments and *thank-you*s.

"Oh, Tem," I said, hugging her so hard I lifted her up, "you were great."

"So were your sets," said Tem.

We stood there, smiling at each other. I wished that Tem and I could go on doing shows together, her singing and me painting, year after year, until we were grown up and life felt solid, and orderly as an outline.

Chapter Twelve

The second show, on Saturday night, went even better. The actors seemed a little more relaxed and a lot more sure of themselves. I tried to hang on to every minute, not wanting it to end. But before we were ready, the final curtain came down. Some of the girls cried because it was over, and the eyeliner ran down their cheeks in long black smudges.

When I got to school Monday morning, Mr. Freeman had posted a notice in the office that all crew members were to meet after school to strike the set.

"What does 'strike the set' mean?" I asked him as I walked onstage.

"It means to take the sets apart and throw them away," he said.

"We can't do that," I said.

"Excuse me, Emma?"

"Well, it's just that my mom's coming back Thursday. I wanted her to see what I painted."

"Sorry," said Mr. Freeman. "The band and orchestra concert is Wednesday. They need the stage area cleared out."

"But . . ." I said.

"Nothing I can do about it," said Mr. Freeman.

"Well, let's get at it," said Ashley, grinning as she grabbed a crowbar from the pile of tools in the center of the stage.

Everything we'd painted—the camels, the tents, the palm trees, all of it—had to be stripped off the support boards and tossed in the Dumpster. The strips of wood were stacked neatly so that they could be used again. Several boys, who had come only once in a while when we were building the sets, showed up to tear them down. They seemed to enjoy all the destruction.

I didn't. I hated every minute. Mr. Freeman showed me how to make a drill run backward to unscrew screws. I messed around with a couple of screws, but my heart wasn't in it. Mostly I wandered around and watched the other kids destroy our beautiful work.

Soon the stage, which had seemed like a magical Old Testament world for so long, was bare.

After the other kids went home, and even Ashley and Christine had left, I sat in the middle of the empty stage and looked out at the empty seats.

Mr. Freeman walked slowly across the stage, his giant feet making no sound.

"You okay?" he asked.

"I guess so," I said.

He knelt down on one knee, next to me. He was looking around too. "That's good," he said. "It's a hard thing to strike a set, to throw away everything you worked on. It makes some people feel sort of empty and alone."

"Empty and alone," I repeated. *This all mattered so much to me and now it's gone.* I thought about next year without Tem. I wondered if all of Northpoint Middle School would feel like an empty stage with the sets taken down.

"You know, though," Mr. Freeman went on, "it's a funny thing, but when I'm done with a project, I'm always ready for the next one. I'm ready to move on, see what surprises are around the corner."

"You mean you're ready to start over?" I asked.

"I sure am," said Mr. Freeman.

I thought about all the fun we'd had. I'd made new friends and learned a lot about theater, which wasn't hard since I hadn't known anything before, and I'd found something I loved to do—work on sets.

"It's like the most fun part is the doing part," I said.

"Exactly," he said. "That's how it is for an artist."

"When I get toward the end of an art project," I admitted, "I'm already thinking about the next one. Sometimes I even rush getting finished. Of course, I've never worked on anything this big before."

"That's it," said Mr. Freeman. "You let go; then it's time to move on." He stood up, walked over, and reached for something he had stored backstage. "Hey, I've got something for you. A souvenir of your first set."

Mr. Freeman had cut out a section of the camel's pack that I had painted. He had mounted it on a piece of BlueGrey posterboard. At the bottom in his perfect printing he had written my name, the date, and *Joseph and the Amazing Technicolor Dreamcoat*.

I knew for certain that when I was as old as Mr. Freeman, I would still have that piece of posterboard.

"Thanks," I said.

I hoped he knew I meant a lot more than one quiet word could say.

Time to move on. I said that to myself about fifty times as I walked home, thinking about all a phrase like that could mean. I decided to find out about

Children's Summer Theater at the park. Maybe there would be a spot for me on the crew. And maybe a spot for Tem in the cast, if she didn't move first.

When I got home, I pushed the front door open with my shoulder because I was holding the posterboard from Mr. Freeman.

"Emma!"

I spun around. Mom was running down the stairs toward me.

She grabbed me in a tight hug. I hugged her back, hoping we weren't bending the posterboard.

"I didn't think you were coming home until Thursday," I said.

"I wanted to surprise you," said Mom. "I missed you so much. Oh, let me get a look at you."

I looked at her too. Mom's long hair was cut short and curly. Her fingernails were bright red. I'd never seen her use even clear polish before.

"Whoa," I said. "What's happened to you?"

Mom smiled. It was her real smile, but she looked sort of shy. "It's my new look, for going back to school. I never went to college before, so this is a big step."

"You look great," I said, trying to decide if she looked younger or older than Mrs. Beauman.

"You look great too," said Mom. "Aunt Grace told me that you two had a marvelous time. She's upstairs packing."

"Mom . . ." I said.

"Oh, and I have a million things to tell you. I brought pictures and postcards and a miniature spoon. I want to hear all about the play. I met some interesting people, but I'll tell you something, it's good to be home."

"Wait a minute," I said. "If you had come home a couple of days earlier, you could have seen the show."

"That's what I wanted to do," Mom said. "But I couldn't get a flight. I was so sorry to miss it. Aunt Grace said your sets were unbelievable."

"Yeah," I said. "They came out pretty good."

"Dad and I can't get over how independent you were, taking on such a big project all on your own," Mom said.

"Well," I said, "I was just part of the crew. Besides, I didn't have much choice. I *was* on my own."

"Great-Aunt Grace was here," Mom pointed out.

"Yeah, she was," I said. "Hey, do you think maybe she could stay a little while longer?"

"Stay here?" asked Mom. "Even though I'm home?"

"Well, don't you have a lot of stuff to tell her?" I asked.

"Great-Aunt Grace?" Mom asked.

"Right," I said. "She'll probably want to hear

all about your trip, and besides, I got kind of used to having her around. Should I ask her if she wants to stay?"

"You can ask her," said Mom doubtfully. "But I think she's packing to leave."

"Be right back," I said, bounding up the stairs.

Great-Aunt Grace was in the guest room, folding her clothes into little bundles. I plopped down on the bed and grabbed her blue scarf, the filmy one she wore to church.

"Can't you stay longer?" I asked her, twisting the scarf around my fingers.

"Afraid not," she said. "My train leaves early tomorrow, at six-thirty A.M. It's called the City of New Orleans."

"I didn't know trains had names," I said.

"This one does, and I'll bet, Miss Emma, there are some other things about the City of New Orleans you don't know either." It was getting dark out, and the light wasn't on in the room, so I couldn't be sure, but I thought she winked at me. Why would she do that? What difference did a train make?

"There'll be a big hole with you gone," I said.

"My apartment is going to seem mighty lonely too," Great-Aunt Grace replied.

"Everything's always changing," I said.

Great-Aunt Grace untangled the scarf that I

had woven in and out of my fingers in a tight knot.

"Let go, Emma," she whispered.

She folded the scarf and put it in the suitcase.

Great-Aunt Grace had this way of making me brave and sort of strong. It was as though she thought I was better than I was, and she wasn't the kind of person to make things up.

Great-Aunt Grace tipped her head back and looked at me. She cleared her throat.

"I was wondering," she said, "if some weekend you'd like to come for a visit. There's a lot we could do in Chicago—art galleries, museums, lunch, so many things."

"Anytime," I said. "All you have to do is call."

Great-Aunt Grace took my hand in her knotted-up old fingers. "You too, Emma—all you have to do is call."

"I know," I said. And I did.

Saying good-bye to Great-Aunt Grace was sad, but it didn't feel scary. It wasn't like she was just leaving me behind. I was already thinking about our first adventure together in Chicago. I'd want to go to the Art Institute. Looking at paintings with Great-Aunt Grace would be interesting, because she'd have more to say than I like this or I don't like that. After the Art Institute, maybe we could go to a hotel for tea, the fancy kind where you got strawberries and whipped cream and little sandwiches with the crusts cut off. Meaghan always talked about doing that when she went shopping with her mom.

Having a friend in Chicago was going to be fun.

Chapter Thirteen

The next day Mom and I got up when it was still dark to make Great-Aunt Grace a send-off breakfast of French toast and two kinds of sausages. Mom thought we were overdoing it, but I insisted.

On the way back from the train station I asked Mom what her plans were.

"Well, I'm all set to start school next week," she said. "The course is called Computer Applications, and it runs for six weeks."

"Will you be fixing dinner every night?" I asked her.

"Of course," said Mom. "The class meets for only two hours a day."

"I need new P.E. shoes," I said.

"Okay," said Mom. "Listen, I just got home. Give me a chance."

"A chance for what?" I said. I was looking straight ahead, through the windshield.

"I don't know," said Mom. "A chance to get things organized, I guess. A chance to make some changes."

"That sounds like a good idea," I said.

"I think so too," said Mom, her voice soft and thoughtful.

We were quiet until we were almost home. I was wondering why my words had sounded mean. Maybe I was still a little bit mad at Mom. For months she had hardly left the couch, and then she flew off to Turkey. Still, I was glad to have her home and all fired up about college. What was the matter with me?

"Oh, and Mom," I said. "One more thing— break a leg."

"What?" said Mom.

"It's theater talk. It means 'good luck,'" I said. "You know, at school."

"Thanks," said Mom. "Thanks a lot. I'll need it. Maybe you should have said 'Break both legs.'"

She laughed. It was a nervous sort of laugh.

The next Monday Tem and I walked straight home after school—no more *Joseph* to work on.

Tem was walking in really slow steps. I had to keep stopping to let her catch up.

"That was a hard math test," I said.

"Yeah," said Tem.

"It's good to have Mom home," I said.

"I bet," said Tem.

"It feels warmer out."

"I guess so."

"Meaghan had on another new outfit."

"Yeah."

"Is something wrong?" I asked.

"No," said Tem.

I stopped and faced Tem and gave her a deep look. Her eyes were worried. She looked like she couldn't laugh even if Meaghan was walking around with a KICK ME sign taped to her back.

"What's up?" I asked.

"Nothing," said Tem.

"You sure?"

"I'm sure."

I let it go. Tem told me stuff when she was ready.

We sat down on my front step. I unzipped my jacket. It was windy but warm for early March.

"Mom's all excited about starting school tomorrow," I said.

"I can't imagine anything exciting about starting a new school," said Tem. "It's big and scary and you don't know anybody. You're lucky. You get to keep everything the same."

"Tem," I said, "you're just plain wrong. I can't seem to keep *anything* the same."

"Well, at least school will stay the same."

"No, it won't," I said. "Every day since kindergarten I've walked to school with you. We have lunch together. We walk home together. We do homework together." I looked at her. "Going to Northpoint without you will be like going to a whole new school."

Tem sighed.

"Want to come in?" I asked.

"Not today," said Tem.

"Okay, bye," I said, and I stood and watched Tem walk down the street, her feet moving as though she had a pound of bubble gum stuck to the bottoms.

Mom was sitting at the kitchen table putting narrow-lined paper into a three-ring binder. She had four mechanical pencils, a pen, and a highlighter in a zipper bag.

"Looks like you're all set for your first day," I said.

"Overready, probably," said Mom. "And nervous. But I want to handle nervousness in the right way."

"What's that mean?" I asked her.

"I think I need to take a walk. Will you come too? You could use your in-line skates."

"Um," I said, "about those in-line skates. They're still in the box. I haven't even tried them on."

"That's okay," said Mom. "You've been too busy. Besides, it's been cold. They probably weren't the most sensible present I ever bought."

I got the skates down from my closet. They fit fine.

Outside, I discovered that I could skate a little but not very fast. My ankles turned in, and I wobbled all over the place.

"Maybe if you held on to me," said Mom.

I held her hand tightly.

"That's better," she said. "We just need a little teamwork."

"Well said," I agreed. We moved along the smooth sidewalks.

"How's Tem?" asked Mom.

"Worried," I said.

"And if I know my Emma," said Mom, "she's worried about Tem being worried."

I couldn't think of much to add to that.

Back home I watched Mom get more nervous by the minute. She started surfing through TV channels at the speed of light. A hundred times she opened the refrigerator door and then shut it without taking anything out. Eventually, worn out from watching her, I headed for my bedroom.

Luckily Dad called that night, to wish Mom

good luck on her first day at school. That calmed her down.

"Do you still remember me?" I asked Dad when it was my turn to talk.

"Of course," he said. "Come on, Emma, you know better than that."

"How much do I weigh? Which side of my nose has a freckle on it?"

He didn't know. I was teasing him, but I was tired of him being gone.

"Are you still coming home the first week in April?" I asked.

"Circle it on the calendar," Dad said. "And have your mom fix a big pan of lasagna."

I made Dad a card. I drew a border of hearts hooked together as though they were holding hands. I colored them scarlet lake, Parma violet, and fuchsia. In the center I wrote:

> *Do you love me*
> *Or do you not?*
> *You told me once*
> *But I forgot.*

I wasn't sure whether I was teasing or not. I mailed it, but the mail wasn't always dependable, just like a lot of things.

Dad was still in Turkey. Mom was nervous. Great-Aunt Grace had left. Tem was moving. I felt as if everything was in a knot, including me.

Chapter Fourteen

Tem wasn't at school. I kept thinking about how worried she'd looked the day before, and I couldn't concentrate on anything. Mrs. Beauman read to us from *Anastasia at Your Service*, and twice the whole class laughed and I didn't even know what they were laughing about.

I got home and all the curtains were closed. *Mom must have a headache*, I thought, opening the front door as quietly as I could.

Standing in the foyer, I could hear crying in the kitchen. I tiptoed across the hall and looked in.

Mom was sitting at the table, books spread all around her, with her head down. Her shoulders shook as she cried.

Oh, no, I thought, *something awful has hap-*

pened to Dad. My heart started pounding so hard I could hear it in my ears.

"Mom," I said, "what is it? What's wrong?"

"Oh, Emma," Mom said, turning toward me, "I just can't do it. Everybody in the class already knows everything about computers. I'm so stupid, I can't even figure out how to pull down those ridiculous menus."

She sobbed a gigantic sob. "I keep letting go of the mouse too soon."

Relief rolled though me so fast, my legs got wobbly and I had to sit down on one of the kitchen chairs.

"My gosh," I said, "you scared me to death."

"Sorry," she said, blowing her nose into a wet tissue.

"I thought something had happened to Dad," I said.

"Dad's fine," said Mom. "It's just me. I'm a stupid-head."

"A stupid-head? Look, I don't know where you come up with these phrases, but you're not stupid."

"I can't even do the mouse," she said, staring at her textbook as if it was a homemade bomb someone had planted on our kitchen table.

I thought about all the times I'd said I couldn't do something—ride a two-wheeler, memorize multiplication tables, get a shot at the doctor's. It seemed as if somebody had always been there saying "Yes, you can." A lot of times that somebody had been Mom.

"Mom," I said, trying to sound grownup, "yes, you can."

"Can what?" she asked, looking up.

"Figure out all this computer stuff," I said.

"But the mouse—"

"Oh, poop on the mouse," I said. "It's easy. I'll teach you. We'll practice together. I'll show you some of my computer games. They'll be fun to use for mouse practice."

"You will?" asked Mom.

"Yep," I said. "I sure will."

"But everybody knows so much more than me," said Mom.

"Everybody in the class can't already know everything about computers, or they wouldn't be taking the course," I said.

Mom blew her nose into that really wet tissue. "Well, maybe everybody doesn't know *everything,* but there was this kid named Franklin Harris, and he was explaining things to the instructor and practically teaching the class."

"Every class has one of those," I said. "I get stuck with Emily Moss in my class every year, and she can do long division in her head. It's just your first day."

"Maybe I'm too old to do this," said Mom. I could hear tears coming back.

"Look," I said, "maybe you just need some help. Justin Finch freaked out about decimals at the beginning of this year and his mom got him a tutor. Now he's in the group that gets to do enrichment packets."

"What?" said Mom.

"A tutor," I said. "Maybe you need a tutor."

"How would I even start trying to find someone?" asked Mom.

"Well," I said, "if it was up to me, I'd start with that Franklin guy."

Mom stared at me. "He's a college kid," she said. "College kids always need money. I could pay him to tutor me."

"There you go," I said.

Mom stood up, walked over, and put her arms around me.

"Thanks, Emma," she said. "I don't know what I'd do without you."

"No problem," I said. I wanted to ask her what was for supper, but that didn't seem like a very good idea. "You'll do fine," I said instead. "The first couple of days are always the worst." I didn't add that tests could be a little tricky too.

The phone rang.

"Emma?" said a voice. "It's Mrs. Temiyasathit. You come over? I think we have the emergency."

I ran as fast as I could. I didn't even knock.

"What is it?" I asked Tem's mom, slipping off my shoes.

"It's Tem," said Mrs. Temiyasathit. "We sold our house and—"

"You sold this house?" I interrupted.

"We sold our house," Mrs. Temiyasathit repeated. "We told Tem last night the contract was finalized, and she fell all into the pieces—cry, cry, cry. All day she lies on the couch like a potato."

Tem's mom sometimes said things in a mixed-up way, but I got the drift. They'd sold the house. Why hadn't we at least tried a couple of ideas from our *Top Ten Ways to Stop the Sale of a House* list? It probably wouldn't have worked anyway—they were all stupid ideas—but we should have at least tried to do *something*. Now it was too late.

"Where's Tem?" I asked.

"In her room," Mrs. Temiyasathit said. "She won't eat anything."

I went upstairs and opened Tem's door. She was asleep. The stuffed frog I'd given her for her sixth birthday stared at me from her pillow. Tem looked little and breakable, like Great-Aunt Grace.

Her room was hot and stuffy. I tiptoed across the carpet. I slid the window open a crack and leaned against the wall. There had to be a way to make this better. What was it Great-Aunt Grace had said the night before she left? There was something I needed to remember. And something else, something that had just happened. Oh, why couldn't I think straight, clear thoughts?

A gust of March wind swooshed in and rattled the pages of a magazine on Tem's desk.

Tem's eyes opened. "You're here," she said.

Right away she started crying. She cried a lot more quietly than Mom.

"Listen up," I said in my Mrs. Beauman voice, "this isn't going to work. Your mom is flipping out. You can't just stay in your room and shrivel up."

Tem sat up in bed and ran her fingers through her hair.

"We're going to go downstairs and we're going to get your mom to fix us something to eat," I said.

"But Emma . . ." Tem said.

"Don't worry," I said. "I'm going to get a plan for us. I'll figure out how we can make this work. It'll be okay."

"Really?" she said.

"Trust me," I said.

Tem smiled as though she did trust me, which made me feel good and bad at the same time. I wanted to make Tem feel better and I'd done that. Maybe saying I was going to get a plan for us would make one magically appear in my mind.

But what if I couldn't? What if I'd just told a big, fat lie to my very best friend?

We went downstairs and had cookies and hot tea with sugar and milk. We talked about all kinds of stuff, but neither of us mentioned the move. And luckily, Tem didn't ask any questions about this wonderful plan I'd said I'd come up with.

About six I walked home. That worried look on Tem's face had been bad enough, but now she trusted me to come up with something. *Think, Emma*, I told myself.

When I got home, Mom was sitting in front of the computer screen with a book in her left hand. She was talking to herself or to the computer, I couldn't tell which. I decided to let her work. I fixed us each a peanut butter and mayonnaise sandwich. I put Mom's plate and a glass of milk next to the computer.

"Thanks, honey," said Mom, looking up. Her eyes were still a little puffy from all the crying.

The phone rang, and this time it was Ashley.

"Hey, Emma," she said. "Christine and I are having a slumber party Friday night, and we're inviting a bunch of the techies from *Joseph*. Mom said we could order three pizzas from three different places and vote on which tastes the best. Then we can watch videos."

"That sounds fun," I said slowly.

"So, you coming?" asked Ashley.

"No," I said. "Thanks for asking. I'm sorry, but I have other plans."

"Well, shoot," said Ashley, and she sounded really disappointed.

"Yeah, shoot," I said back to her.

"Maybe next time," said Ashley.

"Maybe next time," I repeated. "See you later, Ashley."

I hung up the phone.

I knew that somewhere inside of me I *did* want to spend the night at Ashley and Christine's, but I was too worn out to find that feeling. All I could think about was telling Tem that now, on top of everything else, I was invited to a slumber party and she wasn't.

I sat down on the floor next to the phone and started to cry. Who cared if I cried? Tem was upset, but I was there to help. Even if I didn't have a plan yet, I was going to try my hardest to come up with one. That left Tem off the hook. I'd given Mom a good idea about the tutor. I'd get her started, and the tutor could take it from there. Once Mom got going, she'd be okay. Who was there to give *me* any good ideas?

I muffled my crying in my sweatshirt so Mom wouldn't hear. Was crying contagious?

Mom's tears, Tem's tears, my tears. I'd read a story in a book once about a river of tears. I'd thought that was such a stupid phrase, *a river of tears*. Now I wasn't so sure.

Chapter Fifteen

Franklin, the smart kid from Mom's class, agreed to be her tutor. He came every day at three o'clock. He turned out to actually be cute, and not a showoff, which is sometimes a problem with kids like that.

April rolled in and Tem and I pretended that there wasn't a big red SOLD sticker on their FOR SALE sign. We played Monopoly and listened to CDs, and I tried to draw her portrait, but she was terrible at holding still.

Sometimes Tem and I sat in the grass at lunch recess and talked to Ashley and Christine. The three of them—Tem, Ashley, and Christine—got along just fine. Probably they would have let me bring Tem to that slumber party if I had asked. But I hadn't asked and that was that.

The next time, though, would be different. I made up my mind that if I got a chance to do something fun with Ashley or Christine, I was going to say yes.

Franklin taught Mom how to make signs on the computer using "Print Shop." It wasn't a class assignment. It was just for fun.

Mom started slapping signs up everywhere. She made signs for the kitchen cabinets that told what was inside, as if we didn't already know. She made three signs that read TURN OFF THE LIGHTS and one sign she hung inside the front door that asked DO YOU HAVE EVERYTHING YOU NEED? My own bedroom had a sign that read EMMA'S ROOM with a border of crayons. You felt you'd read a chapter by the time you got out the front door.

Mom was getting carried away, but in a good way. She laughed a lot, which made me realize I hadn't heard her laugh in a long time.

Next, Franklin and Mom tackled card making. She stuck cards in my backpack. One said HAPPY APRIL FOOL'S DAY and one said HAPPY BELATED WASHINGTON'S BIRTHDAY. The weirdest one of all said HAPPY FULL MOON.

The night of April tenth, Mom and I taped up a hundred signs that said WELCOME HOME and WE'RE GLAD YOU'RE BACK. We even taped one to the bathroom mirror, which I thought was silly because the steam would wreck it.

Dad was finally coming home.

It's logical that the longer someone is gone, the more excited you'd be that they were coming back. Logical, maybe, but not quite true. When Dad first left, I envisioned the day he would come back as a hundred birthday parties all rolled into one. Even if he had come back at Christmastime, I would have been crazy with excitement. Now something had changed, and that surprised me. Maybe the play had filled up my mind with so many new ideas that there hadn't been room to think as many I-miss-Dad thoughts. Or maybe I was just tired out from so much missing and worry. I couldn't figure it out, but things were different somehow.

I still wound Dad's watch once in a while, especially if I woke up in the night. Sometimes, in my mind, I'd even pretend to talk to him until I fell back asleep. But that hard lump of missing I used to feel all the time had melted.

Still, it would be good to see Dad again.

The next day was a windy, spring-jacket Sunday. We went to pick Dad up at the airport. It wasn't that far, but it seemed to take forever to get there. Would Dad even recognize me? My bangs were all grown out and caught back in my pony-tail. I looked a lot different from my school picture last fall.

Dad walked across the airport carpet in the bright

light, and I realized he looked different too, skinnier and darker. When he first hugged me, I felt my face get hot and I couldn't think of a thing to say.

"What's new, Emma?" he kept asking me on the way home.

I had a hundred things to say, but they were all long stories and I didn't know which one to start with and I didn't think I should start a long story on the way home when he was trying to talk to Mom too. So I kept saying, "Oh, nothing." I was afraid he would think that it didn't matter that he'd been gone so long since I kept saying nothing had happened.

By dinnertime, though, we were talking as if he'd never left.

"Have some more," Mom said, passing Dad the gelatin salad mold. It had little pieces of nuts inside, which I picked out.

"I've had seconds of everything and we've hardly made a dent in all this food," Dad said, smiling.

"I've been cooking for two days," said Mom, smiling back at him.

Leftovers for a week, I thought.

After dinner Dad opened his suitcases. He handed me a Turkish doll, with a heavy red dress and a scarf around her head. The doll's eyes were dark, like Tem's.

"For your collection," he said. Dad always

brought me back a doll when he went to a new country. "Oh, I almost forgot. I picked this up in the airport."

He gave me a bag that said "Kennedy International Airport." Inside was a T-shirt printed with a silver, shimmery Statue of Liberty. It was exactly the right amount of too big.

"I'll wear it tomorrow," I said.

Dad sat in his recliner in the family room and read through a giant stack of my school papers. He even read the report on North Dakota that Tem and I had done so long ago that I'd forgotten about it. I showed him the program from *Joseph* with my name listed in it.

Dad looked at some papers from Mom's class, too. She'd gotten an A on her last test, and Dad was proud of her. I could tell just by the way he held the paper.

"Well," said Dad when he was done reading. "I see you've both managed to do great things, even without me here to cheer you on."

I looked at Mom and grinned.

"So what's next for my two superstars?" asked Dad.

"Lots of homework for me, I'm afraid," said Mom.

"How about you, Emma?" asked Dad. "When does soccer start?"

"Well . . ." I stuttered, my heart speeding up.

"When is the first game?" asked Dad.

I took a deep breath. Then another one. "It's just that I've decided to drop out of soccer."

"Come to think of it," said Mom, "you haven't even mentioned soccer this spring."

"Well, I've decided to quit," I said, and I looked each one of them right in the eyes. "I want to take the Saturday painting classes at the art center instead."

"She's making decisions like this all by herself?" Dad asked Mom, very slowly, as if he was just waking up in the morning.

Before she could answer, I said, "I've talked it over with Ashley and Christine Taylor. We can carpool and the lessons don't cost much."

They were both staring.

"This is important to me. If you leave me on my own, I've got a right to make decisions on my own."

"I'm not sure I know quite what you mean by that, honey," said Mom.

I turned to her.

"Mom, I always do everything you want me to do. I'm where I'm supposed to be, when I'm supposed to be there, and I'm all organized. A lot of times I have to figure stuff out on my own, even when you're home. I deserve a chance to do what I want. And art class is what I want."

They were both watching me, and the house seemed very, very quiet.

"Besides," I added, "you both have to admit I stink at soccer."

"Well, I'd be glad to get more information," said Mom.

"No need," I said. "I've got the dates and times written down. They let me register over the phone."

"Good for you," said Mom, with just a hint of a smile at the corners of her mouth.

"So Emma is making decisions like this all by herself?" Dad seemed a little slow to catch on.

"Yes, she is," I said. "I mean, yes, I am."

"Well," said Dad, "okay by me. You sound like you've thought this through carefully."

"I have," I said.

"Just one big problem, as I see it," said Dad, sounding very ominous. "One very big problem. Huge problem."

"What?" I asked, my heart starting to pound again.

Dad smiled and threw his arms out for a hug. "I want a picture to hang in my office. Can you do that, kid?"

"You've got it," I said.

"And I suppose I'll get stuck doing yard work now on Saturday mornings, instead of relaxing at your soccer games," Dad teased.

"Poor baby," I teased back.

Mom was looking out the family-room window.

"Emma," she said, "you've been a great help to me in my computer class." She turned and looked at Dad. "She really has been, Jim. If she hadn't got me started and talked me into getting Franklin for a tutor, I probably would have quit. Now I'm already signed up for the summer session."

This was news to me.

"So," she said, "what I'm hoping is that I'll be able to help you out with art class, the way you've helped me out with computer class. Maybe sometime this week we can go get your supplies?"

"Okay," I said. "That's my favorite kind of shopping."

I had what I wanted—permission to take art class!

I'd decided on my own and figured it out on my own. I hadn't been looking forward to telling Mom and Dad, but they had been great. Now it was official. I was going to art school.

Not only that, I'd made up my mind to be the best in the class.

Chapter Sixteen

The next day, Monday, Mrs. Beauman handed out the rules for the school's annual Spring Festival Kite Contest, to be held the last Saturday in April. It had been annual twenty-four times, so this year it was an extra-big deal and the winners would get trophies instead of ribbons. There were two prizes for each grade. One was for Most Artistic. The other was for First Up, which meant the first kite to get up into the air.

Tem had been my flying partner every year since kindergarten, but this would be the end. Tem's dad had announced that they were moving to Kankakee as soon as school got out. That left Tem and me about seven weeks to do everything for the last time—a last bicycle ride, a last overnight, a last Spring Festival Kite Contest. There were too many ways we'd have to say good-bye.

I folded my entry form into squares and dropped it into the wastebasket on our way out the classroom door. Tem was right behind me, but she didn't say anything.

In the hallway I practically ran into Mr. Freeman.

"Can't wait to see your kite, Emma," he said. "I bet it'll really be something."

"Oh, yeah, thanks," I said, and he went striding down the hall on his long legs.

Tem unzipped her backpack and handed me her entry form.

"Every year you make a beautiful kite," she said. "So what if it never flies? Maybe this year it will. I still want to be your partner. It's our last shot."

"Don't remind me," I said.

"Listen," Tem went on, "last year you got an honorable mention for Most Artistic. I'll bet you can win in that category this year."

"Okay," I said, "I'll try."

"We'll send that kite into the stratosphere," said Tem.

It was awful hard to say no to Tem.

I drew kite sketches at my desk until bedtime. I laid one sketch after another side by side on my bed. I remembered the day Mr. Freeman had said I had artistic talent. He should know, I figured, since he was an art teacher. It was a favorite thought I kept like a golden coin, and sometimes I picked it up and turned it over and over in my mind.

I thought up so many designs for the kite: a star, a fish, even a dragon. Choosing one was like choosing from the dessert menu at a restaurant— they all looked promising. But I had one idea I couldn't let go of.

Tem and I rode our bikes to the craft store to buy nylon covering and plastic support strips for my kite. Other than that, kites were to be made only of supplies found at home. Mrs. Beauman went over that rule at least fourteen times in class.

"You are not to spend a lot of money on your creation," Mrs. Beauman had said. "Use your imagination, not your allowance."

As we rode home, the spring wind was blowing in our faces, fresh and clean.

"Look!" I shouted ahead to her. "Flowers are poking up all over the place."

"Let's check out our pussy willow," Tem called back over her shoulder.

We left our bikes in Tem's driveway and went around to the back yard. The birds were making a terrible racket. They had left for the winter, like my dad. Now they were back as if nothing had happened, pulling worms out of the chocolate-brown earth and building a subdivision in Tem's cherry tree.

They would leave again in the fall, and I knew sometime my dad would leave again, too. And Tem would leave for Kankakee and never come back. By summer this would be someone else's back yard.

"Look," said Tem, running her fingers along a branch. "The pussy willows are just starting to fuzz out."

"They tickle," I said.

I snapped off a twig and ran it across Tem's face, right under her nose, in that place where you feel how soft things are.

How could Tem and I stay best friends when we didn't see each other every day? I thought about when Monica Holbrook left in second grade because her mom got transferred. Tem and I both promised we'd write and keep in touch, and she said she would, too. The day Monica Holbrook left was the last time either one of us ever heard from her.

"Want some popcorn?" Tem asked.

"Huh?" I asked. "Oh, sure, popcorn sounds good."

We went inside. Tem popped some popcorn in the microwave and divided it into two bowls.

I sprawled out on Tem's bedroom floor with my kite supplies. The white nylon was smooth and fresh as new snow.

Tem flipped the radio to some oldies station and began singing along. The song was about a train called the City of New Orleans and being gone five hundred miles.

"Oh my gosh," I shouted, jumping up. "Now I remember!"

"Remember what?" asked Tem.

I plopped back down. "Let me think," I said, burying my head in my hands. This was one of those ideas I had to grab hold of before it slipped away.

"Think about what?" asked Tem.

I ignored her.

"Emma, you are acting so weird," said Tem after a while.

Finally I pulled my head out of my hands and smiled.

"Tem, old buddy," I said, "I'm finally starting to figure out some plans."

"Plans?" asked Tem.

"Yep," I said. "And these are *real* plans. Not like that dumb list we wrote down before with the dead squirrel and pop in the lawn mower."

"What . . ." Tem said.

"Don't ask," I said. "Not yet."

I was pretty much distracted the rest of the

afternoon. Plan A and Plan B were forming in my mind, one step at a time.

When I left Tem's, I loaded my kite supplies into my backpack and headed downtown, pedaling hard.

I tried to think where I was going. I could always stop and ask for directions. No matter what, I'd find it. I had to pick up a schedule. Plan A was under way.

For Plan B, I needed to talk to Franklin.

Tem stayed home from school the rest of the week with a sore throat. I was busy. Plan A looked very promising. I had what I needed. And Franklin turned out to be a great help. He was checking prices so I could see if Plan B would work.

I spent all my spare time working on the kite. Dad helped me bend the support strips into a heart shape about three feet across. I cut a piece of nylon exactly the same size and glued it to the support strips with a hot-glue gun.

I drew a jagged line down the middle of the heart, just like the jagged line down the heart pendants Tem had bought us for Christmas. Every day I wore the half a heart that said "Best," and every day Tem wore the half that said "Friends."

At least on my kite the two halves were together with nothing separating them.

I colored two-inch squares of nylon with my markers and glued them all over the kite, as close together as I could get them. I glued one end down, leaving the other end free. They were like fish scales, and my plan was that they would catch the sun and shimmer and wave in the wind. It felt good to take each small piece and glue it to a place where it would stay put.

One half of the heart I did in sea colors: aquamarine, lime, teal blue, and royal peacock, which was the color of my eyes.

The other side had scales of burnished gold, iridescent copper, and burnt sienna. I called them Marco Polo colors, the colors of the Orient.

The night I glued on the last square, Mom and Dad came in to say good night.

"Emma," said Dad, "this is no kite. This is a work of art."

"Dad's right," said Mom. "After the kite contest, let's hang it from your ceiling. I really am impressed, honey."

"Me too," said Dad, "whether it flies or not."

That night I was too tired to fall asleep. I tried to think about happy things, but worries kept flying into my mind like moths crashing into our porch light. What would happen to me next year without Tem? Would Mom do okay at school? Would Dad leave again soon? And, most of all, would my Plan A and Plan B be good enough to keep Tem and me best friends? I wanted to have every detail of both plans figured out before I said anything. That way, telling Tem about my plans would be like giving her a present.

When I finally fell asleep, I dreamed that a fifty-foot-tall dragon, with blue and copper scales, was stalking through the neighborhood. He filled the middle of the street. With his watery red eyes he peered down through bedroom windows searching for a victim, hungry for a child to snatch away.

Chapter Seventeen

The morning of April twenty-fourth, the day of the Spring Festival Kite Contest, I stuck my head outside the kitchen door. The air was cool, and I couldn't see one cloud in a sky the color of my cerulean blue marker.

"We'll head over to the park," said Mom. "Dad had an appointment at the office, so he's going to meet us there."

"We're picking Tem up," I said.

"That's fine," said Mom. "I'll bet your kite wins Most Artistic. I can't imagine a prettier one. Will it fly?"

"They never do," I said.

The contest was held in the city park, which was a great place for kite flying. The ground lay flat as a pancake below a ridge, like a giant earth bowl. This kept the wind from being too strong for launching.

Mom popped the trunk so I could get the kite. I had wrapped it in a big garbage bag, and I suddenly felt shy about taking it out.

Tem and I walked over to the judges' table to sign in. Mr. Freeman was there. He took my kite out of the bag gently and looked at it for a long time.

"This is a great job, Emma," Mr. Freeman said finally. "It's up to your usual standard."

"Thanks," I said, feeling that warm-honey feeling again.

"Guess what," Mr. Freeman said. "I've decided to get the art club going. We'll meet every Wednesday until school lets out, so we have something to build on next year."

"That sounds great," I said.

"I'd like you to work with Ashley and Christine on a design for a poster contest. Think you'll have time?"

"You bet," I said, wondering a hundred things already, like would we use paint or markers and what size, and what kind of paper. "I can't wait to get started."

The judges nodded to each other as they examined my kite. They made notes on a canary yellow form. I looked at Tem. She looked worried.

Behind me I heard a familiar voice. Meaghan had arrived. She charged over and grabbed my kite.

"A heart!" exclaimed Meaghan. "Oh, my gosh, Emma, you made your kite look like those necklaces you and Tem wear."

"Meaghan," I said, "I'm impressed. You are so observant. To tell you the truth, I didn't think anybody would put all that together."

"I would," said Meaghan. "I look at your necklaces all the time. I mean, you wear them every single day."

"Yeah, we do," I said, imagining myself in a white dress, getting married, still wearing my half-a-heart necklace. "And we always will," I added.

"No doubt," said Meaghan, "nothing will ever change your perfect little friendship. Neither one of you will ever need another friend."

Something about the way she was talking made me wonder if Meaghan wished she had a best friend.

"Where's your kite?" I asked, changing the subject.

"Check this out," said Meaghan. She reached into a fancy canvas bag and pulled out this incredible mass of bright-pink, rippling, floaty feathers.

"What the heck . . ." stammered Tem.

"What is it?" I asked.

Then we got it. Meaghan, and no doubt her mother, had constructed a kite that resembled a life-size, full-feathered, pinker-than-pink flamingo. Its head stuck up above and its legs hung down below, and the main part of the kite was a solid flamingo-pink mass of fluttering, quivering feathers.

"You just happened to have a bushel of flamingo feathers lying around your house, Meaghan?" I asked.

"Of course not," said Meaghan. "These feathers were special-ordered, from New York City."

I said, "But that's . . ."

"I know," said Meaghan, looking down at her new pink tennis shoes. "But tell my mom."

I looked at Meaghan's mom, who was talking to the judges. She had on a ton of gold jewelry. Why did she do all this stuff? Most kids had parents you could hardly tell apart. Meaghan's mom looked ready to anchor the six o'clock news.

"Meaghan," she said dramatically, "let's find our launching spot, shall we, dear?"

Poor Meaghan. That flamingo kite was more over the top than the costume she'd had to wear as Potiphar's wife. And she had nobody to help her launch her kite but her mom.

"Good luck, Meaghan," I said, holding out my hand.

She took it. Her fingers were tiny.

"Thanks," she said, in a voice her mom couldn't

hear. "Your heart is pretty. Everybody knows you're one of the best artists in the school."

"They do?" I said.

But Meaghan had already turned and was walking away with her mom, who was barking out orders about how to launch a kite.

"I wouldn't switch places with her," I said.

"I know," said Tem. "And on top of everything else, I don't think that flamingo would fly in a wind tunnel."

"Speaking of flying," I said, "it's time."

"Wait," said Tem. "I haven't said anything about your kite yet, about how it's like our necklaces and everything. But I noticed too. I noticed right away."

"What were you going to say?" I asked her.

"That's just it," said Tem. "I don't know what to say." Tem shrugged her shoulders, and her eyes filled with tears.

"Know what?" I said.

"What?" said Tem.

"Sometimes the only words people think of to say are dumb words, like the ones on posters or bookmarks."

"And?"

"And so not knowing what to say is a lot smarter than saying dumb words."

"Thanks," said Tem.

"You're welcome," I said. "Let's go."

Chapter Eighteen

Tem and I walked out to the center of the park. I stood with the wind at my back. Tem took my kite and walked a long way downwind. I held the line firmly so there was no slack. The breeze blew my hair forward.

The starting gun for fifth grade went off, and Tem let go.

My kite, my beautiful heart kite, rose like an eagle headed for the sky. The line stayed taut, rapidly unwinding from the spool in my hands. Higher and higher my kite soared, slapped up against the cloudless sky.

I saw Tem jumping up and down, cheering. The wind carried her voice away, but I knew what she was saying. We were first up! The sun caught the

scales on the heart, and they glimmered and sparkled in the cool, clear air.

Other kites were headed upward too, but already my kite, Tem's and mine, was the highest. The other kites were every color of the rainbow, and they darted and bobbed all around my kite like a giant sky mobile.

I heard laughter behind me. I turned and looked. It was time for the sixth-grade launch. Ashley and Christine were throwing their kite up into the air, but it kept crashing back down. They didn't seem to be taking it too seriously. Behind them Meaghan and her mom were holding a mass of pink feathers. They were yelling at each other— I could tell by the way their heads were tilted.

I scanned the crowd, looking for Mom and Dad. I spotted Mom. I made the number-one sign with my index finger to show we were first up. Where was Dad? He had to be there. I looked at everybody and then I looked again.

I couldn't find him.

Where was Dad for my big moment? How could he miss this? The line kept spinning off my spool, and I stood there with cement in my arms, unable to move a finger.

Tem was walking toward me.

"Hang on!" she yelled into the wind.

"No," I said softly. The line was pulling out,

faster and faster. It felt good. I was tired of hanging on so tight. Hanging on for Mom to keep her act together, hanging on for Dad to get home and stay home, hanging on to Tem. I was tired of everyone leaving and tired of trying to hold on to them. I was tired of trying to keep everything the same.

"Grab the string!" yelled Tem.

I reached out with my right hand and grabbed the string. I felt it pulling through my hand, but I couldn't bring myself to hold the string tightly enough to stop it. Tears ran down my face, and the wind took them and the sound of my crying.

I scanned the crowd. Mom was pointing to Dad, who was running up the ridge to stand next her. His tie flapped in the wind like the tongue of an eager dog. He waved at me, all smiles. But he'd missed it. He missed my big first-up moment, just as he'd missed my soccer games, and *Joseph*, and a hundred other things.

My kite was soaring farther and farther away. Unwinding off the spool, the string ran through my hand, cutting into my palm. The string was taut and straight, straight as the line between my house and Tem's house had always been. It was unraveling.

"Emma!" said Tem, about an inch from my face. "Stop!"

She put her hand on top of mine and squeezed. The line stopped going out. The kite stayed where it was, pasted like a postage stamp against the sky.

We stood there, together, her hand over mine. The wind blew all around us and Tem's hand held my hand and my hand held the string.

"I don't know what to do," said Tem at last. "I'm afraid to leave you. I don't know who I'll be if you're not my best friend. I'm scared."

She didn't need to tell me she was scared. Tem looked more frightened than I'd ever seen her look in all the years and years we'd been looking in each other's faces.

It had to stop. I had to make it better.

"I'll be your best friend," I told her. "That's for always."

"But I won't see you," said Tem, with a sound in her voice like the beginning of tears.

"Listen, Tem," I said. "I told you I had some things worked out. I wanted to wait until I had every single detail perfect, but I think I should tell you now. Remember that day I bolted out of your room? I went to the train station and picked up a schedule. That's our Plan A."

"What is?" asked Tem.

"The train," I said. "There's this train called the City of New Orleans. It's the one Great-Aunt Grace takes when she comes to visit."

"So?" asked Tem.

"So," I said, "it also makes stops in Champaign

and Kankakee. It's only about an hour's ride, from here to there, and it doesn't cost much at all."

"Oh, my gosh, the train," said Tem, her eyes hinting at a smile. "Do you think our parents would let us?"

"I bet yours would. Mom already said I could ride the train up to see you. She also says she'll drive me to your house sometimes, but the train is our backup plan. We can set that up ourselves. We don't have to count on anybody to help us with that."

"That's a good idea," said Tem. "It makes Kankakee sound not so far away."

"That's only half of it," I said. "Plan B is E-mail."

"E-mail?" asked Tem.

"Yeah," I said. "I talked to Franklin, and he showed me how easy it's going to be for us to E-mail each other on our computers."

"But it'll cost . . ." said Tem.

"No," I said, "that's the thing. It's cheap, once we get set up, nothing like using the phone to call long distance. We can earn the money ourselves if we have to, baby-sitting or something."

"So I can come home from school every day and E-mail you?" asked Tem.

"Exactly," I said. "And I'll E-mail you back. I'll do separate stuff and you'll do separate stuff, and the together part will be when we tell each other about it."

"It'll help," said Tem.

"It'll be okay," I said. And I knew it would be. Not perfect. Not the way I wanted it. But okay.

"We can try to make the best of it," said Tem.

"Yep," I said. "It's like my Great-Aunt Grace told me once. You have to play the notes on the page, but how you play them is up to you. It took me a while to figure out what she meant."

"Should we reel the kite in?" said Tem.

"Not just yet," I said. "You go on back and get our trophy. I want to stand here for a while."

I was going to give Tem the trophy, as a souvenir. We'd won the kite contest. Maybe we'd won something else too.

I looked over at the judges' stand. Mr. Freeman was sitting there. I was going to see him Wednesday afternoon when the art club met. Meaghan and her mom were scrambling around like crazy, picking up pink feathers that covered the ground like a cotton candy snowfall. Poor Meaghan.

Ashley and Christine were still trying to get their kite into the sky, and they were laughing because it kept dive-bombing into the dirt.

Tem had picked up our trophy, and she was holding another trophy as well. I must have won Most Artistic! She was showing them to Mom and Dad, who were smiling at me like crazy. Dad stuck out both arms with his thumbs up. I checked out the crowd. I didn't see a lot of dads. *Maybe he was late, but at least he came.*

A breeze, way up high, tugged at my kite, and the string began unwinding again. What had Mr. Freeman said? *It's time to move on.* My kite was moving on.

I let it run. Everything was so beautiful—the sky, my kite, Tem and my parents acting as though I'd just won the Olympics. I took the deepest breath.

I could see Tem pointing up to my kite. It was now just a bright, shimmering spot in the perfect blue sky. It kept pulling away, riding on the wind. The spool was almost empty. I watched it unwind.

I cupped my hand around the string and felt it pass through my fingers. I let go, and the kite took it all—string and spool—up into the sky.

With nothing in my hands, I turned and ran, toward whatever came next, toward the people who were cheering just for me.

About the Author

Nancy Steele Brokaw is a freelance journalist who has written for both children and adults. She has drawn from many of her own experiences in writing *Leaving Emma,* her first novel. "When I was a kid, my dad traveled a lot and my best friend moved away. I think a few of Emma's feelings were still inside me, but Emma is her own person. I was proud of her by the end of the story," she says. Nancy Steele Brokaw lives with her family in Illinois.